THE
METROPOLITAN
OPERA
MURDERS

HELEN TRAUBEL

Published by Poisoned Pen Press, an imprint of Sourcebooks,
in association with the Library of Congress
P.O. Box 4410, Naperville, Illinois 60567-4410
(630) 961-3900
sourcebooks.com

This edition of *The Metropolitan Opera Murders* is based on the first edition in the Library of Congress's collection, originally published in 1951 by Simon and Schuster.

Library of Congress Cataloging-in-Publication Data

Names: Traubel, Helen, author. | Klinger, Leslie S., editor.
Title: The Metropolitan Opera murders / Helen Traubel ; edited, with an
   introduction and notes, by Leslie S. Klinger.
Description: Naperville, Illinois : Poisoned Pen Press in association with
   the Library of Congress, 2022. | Series: Library of Congress crime
   classics | "This edition of The Metropolitan Opera Murders is based on
   the first edition in the Library of Congress's collection, originally
   published in 1951 by Simon and Schuster." | Includes bibliographical
   references.
Identifiers: LCCN 2021037057 (print) | LCCN 2021037058 (ebook) | (trade paperback) | (epub)
Subjects: LCSH: Opera--Fiction. | Metropolitan Opera (New York,
   N.Y.)--Fiction. | LCGFT: Detective and mystery fiction. | Novels.
Classification: LCC PS3539.R273 M48 2022 (print) | LCC PS3539.R273
   (ebook) | DDC 813/.54--dc23
LC record available at https://lccn.loc.gov/2021037057
LC ebook record available at https://lccn.loc.gov/2021037058

Printed and bound in the United States of America.
SB 10 9 8 7 6 5 4 3 2 1

CONTENTS

FOREWORD

Crime writing as we know it first appeared in 1841, with the publication of "The Murders in the Rue Morgue." Written by American author Edgar Allan Poe, the short story introduced C. Auguste Dupin, the world's first wholly fictional detective. Other American and British authors had begun working in the genre by the 1860s, and by the 1920s we had officially entered the golden age of detective fiction.

Throughout this short history, many authors who paved the way have been lost or forgotten. Library of Congress Crime Classics bring back into print some of the finest American crime writing from the 1860s to the 1960s, showcasing rare and lesser-known titles that represent a range of genres, from cozies to police procedurals. With cover designs inspired by images from the Library's collections, each book in this series includes the original text, reproduced faithfully from an early edition in the Library's collections and complete with strange spellings and unorthodox punctuation. Also included are a contextual introduction, a brief biography of the author, notes, recommendations for further reading, and suggested discussion questions. Our hope is for these books to start conversations, inspire further research, and bring obscure works to a new generation of readers.

Early American crime fiction is not only entertaining to read, but it also sheds light on the culture of its time. While many of the titles in this series include outmoded language and stereotypes now considered offensive, these books give readers the opportunity to reflect on how our society's perceptions of race, gender, ethnicity, and social standing have evolved over more than a century.

More dark secrets and bloody deeds lurk in the massive collections of the Library of Congress. I encourage you to explore these works for yourself, here in Washington, DC, or online at www.loc.gov.

—Carla D. Hayden, Librarian of Congress

INTRODUCTION

Crime fiction and thrillers have been published under the names of celebrities of all types, including presidential children Susan Ford, Margaret Truman,* and Elliott Roosevelt, vice presidential spouse Marilyn Quayle, and, most recently, President Bill Clinton, as well as journalist William F. Buckley Jr., actors William Shatner and Helen Hayes, and various sports stars.† Some celebrities have published mysteries to burnish their credentials as intelligent, perhaps enhancing their public image; others seem to have done so just for fun.

Until the 1940s, however, few performers wrote or lent their

---

* In an odd twist, Helen Traubel spent three years coaching Margaret Truman, who pursued a singing career.

---

† Dick Francis (1920–2010), it should be noted, who was a famous steeplechase jockey before he published his first novel in 1962, had a highly successful career as a mystery novelist and journalist for nearly forty years; certainly, while many of his fans appreciated his intimate knowledge of the racing world, few remembered his own athletic career in the 1950s.

names to mysteries.* The first notable success was burlesque queen Gypsy Rose Lee, who was named as the author of *The G-String Murders* (1941) and *Mother Finds a Body* (1942). Though focused on the theatrical world of vaudeville familiar to Lee, both were ghostwritten by the highly successful mystery writer Craig Rice.† Rice also co-ghosted the suave actor George Sanders's *Crime on My Hands* (1944), a comic mystery involving a movie production. Sanders's name also appeared on *Stranger at Home* (1946), ghosted by Leigh Brackett,‡ though the book had little do with Sanders or his insider's knowledge other than a Southern California locale. The swashbuckling actor Errol Flynn was credited as the author of a novel published in Australia in 1946 called *Showdown*, purportedly based on his own early adventures as a youth in New Guinea.

The amount of credit claimed by the celebrities has varied over time, seemingly without reference to the extent contributed by the celebrity to the project. For example, the Lee books did not hint at their coauthorship. The Sanders novels included dedications to the ghostwriters, though the marketing hyped the stories as reflecting Sanders's personality. Other celebrities have included

---

* Harry Houdini was a notable exception. Expanding beyond his stage performances as a magician and escapologist, Houdini starred in a number of adventure films, in which he portrayed a figure of action, usually a spy. His name also appeared as the byline for a number of short stories. The best known is the story "Imprisoned with the Pharaohs" (also known as "Under the Pyramids"), published in *Weird Tales* for May/June/July 1924 and written by H. P. Lovecraft. When the story was reprinted in 1939 (after Houdini's death), the editor noted that Houdini had "dictated" the story to a stenographer but that it had been written by Lovecraft. Other works credited to Houdini were ghostwritten by Walter Gibson, creator of the Shadow, and probably by Fulton Oursler.

---

† The pseudonym of Georgiana Ann Randolph Craig (1908–1957), whose twenty-one mystery novels are a brilliant combination of screwball comedy and noir soaked in alcohol.

---

‡ Brackett (1915–1978), known as the "Queen of Space Opera," was a well-regarded science fiction writer and screenwriter. She is credited for work on *The Big Sleep* (1946), *Rio Bravo* (1959), and *The Long Goodbye* (1973). Brackett also worked on an early draft of *The Empire Strikes Back* (1980).

the coauthor in acknowledgments. Occasionally, a professional writer received public credit with a byline in smaller letters. By contrast, Bill Clinton gave equal credit to James Patterson (who may be as big a celebrity as Clinton).*

Helen Traubel, the leading soprano at the Metropolitan Opera and one of the most famous women of the late 1940s to early 1950s, was a great fan of mystery fiction, but she was not the first opera star to write mystery fiction. That credit belongs to Queena Marian Tillotson (1896–1951), professionally known as Queena Mario, who sang more than three hundred times at the Met between 1922 and 1938. Tillotson began as a journalist, and as her singing career declined, she returned to writing. She published three opera-themed murder mysteries (now long out of print): *Murder in the Opera House* (1934), *Murder Meets Mephisto* (1942), and *Death Drops Delilah* (1944).†

Traubel did not share Tillotson's journalist background, but in 1949, she tried her hand at writing, penning a short novel called *The Ptomaine Canary*. *Time* magazine, which called the novel "improbable even by whodunit standards," suggested that Traubel had taken up writing to fill empty hours:

> *Soprano Traubel had written her 5,500-word, six-installment mystery in dressing rooms and train compartments while on tour last fall. Unlike her heroine, Soprano Traubel had to drug nobody to get her story before the public. The Associated Press*

---

* Their second novel together, *The President's Daughter*, was published in the summer of 2021.

---

† All were published by the venerable E. P. Dutton & Company, and there was at least a second printing of her first book. *Murder Meets Mephisto* was also published by the *Philadelphia Inquirer* as a "Gold Seal" novel (a supplement to the newspaper) and reprinted as a paperback in 1945. However, Tillotson was not nearly as well known as Traubel: Traubel's death, nineteen years after she last sang for the Met, was front-page news in the *New York Times*, while Tillotson's death was noted only on the obituary page.

*heard about it, [and] snapped it up for distribution to the
200-odd papers which regularly use its serial-story service.**

The popularity of her short mystery led to a second effort, a
full-length novel. This time, however, Traubel (or Lee Wright, her
editor at Simon & Schuster†) brought in a ghostwriter, a forty-
year-old lawyer named Harold Q. Masur (1909–2005), who was
building his own distinguished career as a mystery writer. Masur
had only published his first novel in 1947, the hard-boiled *Bury
Me Deep* featuring lawyer Scott Jordan, but he had a solid track
record writing short stories for the pulp magazines in the early
1940s. This was apparently Masur's only venture as a ghostwriter,
and he never mentioned it in interviews. The protagonist of
Metropolitan Opera Murders couldn't have been more different
from Masur's lawyer/tough guy hero, but his sense of humor must
have meshed with Traubel's. Masur had a long and successful
career, with his last book published in 1981.‡ He was a founder
of the Mystery Writers of America and served as its president in
1973; for many years thereafter, he served as its general counsel.

The Metropolitan Opera was arguably the most famous opera
company in the world, and its weekly radio broadcasts made
opera—and Traubel—familiar to millions of Americans. Traubel's
name on the cover suggested insider gossip about the storied
venue and its stars, and *The Metropolitan Opera Murders* was
therefore much anticipated. When the book appeared, however,

---

* "Music: Murder at the Met?" *Time*, April 24, 1950.

---

† Wright was the editor of the long-running Inner Sanctum mystery series published by
Simon & Schuster beginning in 1930. The popular series inspired a hit radio show of
the same name between 1941 and 1952, producing more than five hundred episodes of
creepy stories, as well as films and a television series. At the end of each radio episode,
the latest book in the Inner Sanctum series was announced. Wright was also responsible
for publishing Craig Rice, Gypsy Rose Lee, and Anthony Boucher, among others.

---

‡ His output is set forth in Further Reading, page 189.

some reviewers were not kind. *Kirkus Reviews,* for example, said: "As a crime baffler, it is definitely second rate."* Others were more positive: "Miss Traubel's choice of background," wrote Richard S. Hill for the journal of the Music Library Association, "intensifies murder's intrinsic horror through the logical employment of glamorous characters at the same time that it makes the murders completely credible. The result, although hardly a classic of the genre, should divert most musicians well enough."† The book sold moderately—it was a choice of the Inner Sanctum series and mentioned on other recommended reading lists—but Traubel had had her lark and did not return to writing.

The Metropolitan Opera Murders remains enjoyable today for the simple reason that the world of opera has not changed, perhaps in over 150 years. We are captured by its glamor, intrigued by its passions, and comforted that here is the real deal—a story told by not only an insider but *the* insider of the age, perhaps the best-known American opera singer of her time. The book bucked the trend of hard-boiled, noir-inspired fiction and found its place in another sphere of crime fiction, the cozy mystery, in which bad things happen largely out of the reader's purview, the crimes are relatively bloodless, and good people prevail. One can comfortably imagine Traubel, a most genial personality, telling the story about her troubles and how she and her friends worked them out.

Read this charming book, then, not for its psychological depths or intricate mysteries but rather to visit a magical place backstage, in the company of an expert with a sense of humor and an unerring eye for detail. Brava, Ms. Traubel!

—Leslie S. Klinger

---

* "Review of *The Metropolitan Opera Murders,*" *Kirkus Reviews,* October 5, 1951, https://www.kirkusreviews.com/book-reviews/a/helen-traubel /the-metropolitan-opera-murders/.

---

† *Notes* 9, no. 1 (December 1951): 135.

CHAPTER ONE

Opera singers are a notoriously strange breed, tempestuous, temperamental, erratic. When a group of them assemble on stage for a performance anything is likely to happen—and frequently does.

But never, in all its eventful history, had the Metropolitan* witnessed anything like the catastrophe which befell Rudolf Salz on that particular Wednesday afternoon during the second act of Richard Wagner's *Die Walküre.*†

---

* The Metropolitan Opera is both a place and a company of performers. Founded in 1883, it was originally housed at Thirty-Ninth and Broadway in Manhattan. It quickly became a venue for the greatest stars of opera from around the world and, like many opera houses, established its own repertory company with a core of regular performers and featured stars. The Met joined with other theatrical companies in 1966 in moving to the Lincoln Center in Manhattan, where it remains. In 1931, the Met broadcast an entire opera on the radio, and soon thereafter, regular Saturday afternoon broadcasts made the Metropolitan Opera accessible to millions of listeners around the globe, many of whom could neither travel to New York nor afford to purchase tickets. By 1951, the Met was arguably the best-known opera company in the world.

---

† Richard Wagner (1813–1883) was a prolific composer of opera, with thirteen to his credit. The second of Wagner's *Der Ring des Nibelungen* (The Ring of the Nibelung) cycle, *Die Walküre* (The Valkyrie), was completed in 1856 and first performed in 1870. In Wagner's story, Siegmund and Sieglinde, twin children of Wotan, are separated as infants but reunited as adults, unknown to each other. They fall in love and have a child. Brünnehilde, another child of Wotan, saves them from the wrath of the gods. The opera clocks in at four hours, a real test of stamina for performers and audiences alike. Like Elsa, Traubel herself played Brünnehilde numerous times, including with Max Lorenz as Siegmund and Rose Bampton as Sieglinde in a performance at the Met on February 10, 1950.

It happened right in front of the soprano's eyes. Salz, strictly speaking, was not a member of the company. At the moment, however, he was filling a job in the prompter's box. And Elsa Vaughn, singing Brünnehilde, with her voice soaring over a flaming volcano of music from the orchestra pit, could not believe what she saw. Rudolf Salz, without warning, had suddenly begun to make faces at her.

Not just comical faces, but horrible distortions that kept pulling his features grotesquely out of shape. It was incredible. Salz, once a famous *Heldentenor*,* once the idol of Bayreuth,† a man who had lived for and by music, now seemed bent on ruining the performance.

It must be a trick of lighting, Elsa Vaughn tried to tell herself. A trick of lighting conjured up by the klieg lamps‡ that illuminated the setting—a wild and craggy mountain pass with jagged rocks running along both sides of the stage.

She was singing to Karl Ecker, the season's new tenor, promising him happiness in Valhalla, when Salz began his amazing performance. Ecker, in his coarse gray tunic covered with shaggy fur, was himself staring at the prompter. But he managed to look away and catch Elsa's eye in an effort to keep her going.

---

* According to the *Oxford English Dictionary*, "[A person with a] powerful tenor voice suited to the singing of heroic roles in opera." It is a vocal category specifically associated with the works of Richard Wagner. Wagner's writing for the tenor voice requires power in the middle and lower register that was not typical in other operas of the time.

---

† A town in Bavaria, Bayreuth has been since 1876 the site of an annual music festival devoted to the works of Wagner, regarded as the greatest of all German opera composers. The festival is held in the Richard Wagner Festspielhaus, an opera house designed by Wagner and funded by Ludwig II of Bavaria, intended to be an ideal acoustic space for the performance of his own operas. During World War II, the festival continued under Nazi sponsorship (Adolf Hitler was very fond of the works of Wagner and saw them as embodying German ideals), until much of Bayreuth was bombed. The festival did not resume as a Wagner-themed event until July 1951.

---

‡ Originally, a specific brand of arc lamp used in moviemaking, but now more generally any powerful electrical theatrical lighting. The Metropolitan Opera House was one of the first New York theaters to employ Klieg lighting.

The attempt failed. Her voice faltered, lost the beat, and went flat.

Rudolf Salz had suddenly shot upright, thumping his head against the metal hood that concealed him from the audience. A convulsive spasm shook his body. Both hands clutched at his throat. His face turned blue, and his tongue, swollen and discolored, came out between his teeth. His eyes, red-veined and wild, were fixed on Elsa. Then, very slowly, he began to disappear. He went sliding and bumping down the six iron steps that led into the basement.

Elsa gasped. There had been something terrifying in Rudolf Salz's gaze, in his terrible accusing stare. Perhaps it was only natural that her next note was a full octave off pitch. That she was able to continue at all was a minor triumph. Instinct and years of training helped.

So did Frederick Koch, the conductor. At this point, Koch was responsible for the smoothness of the performance. He held her eyes, and his baton, aimed like a threat, quivered with authority. His chin was up and his mouth was grim. His gestures, crisp and commanding, brought her back and fused her voice to the orchestra.

Then, mercifully, Karl Ecker, as Siegmund, took over. A tall man with a sharply boned face and the great barrel chest of a Wagnerian tenor, he sang his defiance to Wotan's orders. While his voice seemed to ring out clear and sure, there were those in the audience among the cognoscenti who were able to detect a faint tremolo in its upper register. This too was only natural. Not even a Wagnerian tenor can observe with equanimity a man dying before his eyes.

And Rudolf Salz was dead.

Of that there was no doubt. They had seen his face, just before he disappeared from sight, haunted and agonized.

Music swelled out of the orchestra pit, the music of Richard Wagner in all its prodigal and opulent beauty. But no one backstage was listening. Stagehands, electricians, supers, and *Walküre* all made a concerted rush toward the basement.

There, on the concrete floor, they found Rudolf Salz. His gaunt face was still and relaxed, one leg was twisted clumsily under the other, and both arms were flung out in a helpless, supplicating gesture.

CHAPTER TWO

There are certain extremists who consider the Metropolitan as one of our last bastions of culture, a bulwark against the onslaught of comic books, soap operas, and television. And it is quite true that music is an elevating medium. It is also true that some of the old-line boxholders continue to celebrate each performance as a social event in which to exhibit their sables, coiffures, and escorts. But the vast majority of listeners are true lovers of music drama. They attend with regularity and devotion, and their enthusiasm thunders over the bravos of professional claques. No other type of entertainment produces such explosive ovations.

The reception for this afternoon's performance of *Die Walküre*, however, was mixed and uncertain. What had promised to be a memorable performance when it started had suddenly and unaccountably become rather pale and inept. The audience poured out of the exits feeling puzzled and uncomfortable.

This reaction was nothing compared to that of the management. The Metropolitan is a unique institution. A lodestone drawing great artists from all parts of the world. No breath of scandal must be permitted to tarnish its name. And the management recognizes this responsibility. So of course the murder of Rudolf Salz shook the old structure to its foundation.

For murder it was.

Detective-Lieutenant Sam Quentin* reached this conclusion immediately upon arrival. The evidence indicated poisoning by strychnine,† confirmed later by a report from the Medical Examiner. The strychnine had been introduced into Salz's stomach through the medium of a bottle of scotch whiskey, found in the victim's pocket.

Lieutenant Quentin was a new-generation cop. Tall, well-mannered, well-tailored, precise. He had penetrating blue eyes and a deceptively mild voice. Competence had lifted him to his present position of authority while dogged independence prevented him from rising higher.

His first act had been to seal off the entire backstage area, allowing no one to leave. Seated now at the desk of the managing director, he swiveled back and looked up at the man whose chair he had usurped. "You say that Salz does not work here. Then what was he doing in the prompter's box?"

Aaron Van Cleff looked harassed and unhappy. As the man charged with the artistic destinies of the Met, he possessed neither the temperament nor the fortitude to cope with an event of this nature. Thin, sensitive, with a halo of white hair over a high-boned forehead, he kept folding and unfolding his hands in a continuous nervous gesture.

"Our regular prompter took sick," he explained. "We had to send him home. Salz was backstage and I asked him to fill in. It was an emergency. He knew as much about Wagnerian

---

* This is the first hint of Traubel's sense of humor—"Sam Quentin" is remarkably close to the well-known California penitentiary San Quentin. And a wealthy family named DeBrett (the well-known guide to English manners and peerage) and an opera manager named Van Cleff (the musical notation)? Traubel may well have intended the book to parody the hard-boiled detective novels popular at the time.

† A highly toxic vegetable alkaloid, used in medicine as a stimulant. Today it is primarily used in the US for underground eradication of vermin.

opera as anyone alive. In Europe he was a great *Heldentenor* before—"

"A what?" Quentin was puzzled.

"*Heldentenor*. Heroic tenor. A singer who specializes in Wagnerian roles."

The Lieutenant's activities had left him little time for the pursuit of musical knowledge. But he had listened to an occasional Saturday afternoon broadcast and he had a rather vague notion of German opera as all sound and fury.

"Go on about Salz," he said.

"Salz was singing in Cologne;* he was a great favorite when the war broke out." Van Cleff spread his hands. "The Nazis grabbed him and confiscated his property and threw him into a concentration camp."

"Why?"

"Politics. Salz was too free with his tongue. An artist cannot live in an ivory tower." Van Cleff lifted his shoulders. "Anyway, I don't have to tell you what it was like. After three years there was nothing left. Salz was only a shell, his voice gone, his money gone, everything—all that remained was his knowledge. He came to America and started to teach."

"Many pupils?"

"Unfortunately, no. At one time or another he has coached every singer of major importance in the German repertory. But teaching is a difficult profession and Salz's attitude militated against it. He was an embittered man."

"Was this his regular hangout?"

"Only for performances of Wagner. Hilda Semple,† who sang

---

* The Cologne (Germany) Opera Company was established in 1822 and has a worldwide reputation.

---

† The name is another musical joke: Frieda Hempel (1885–1955) was a highly regarded German soprano, known for her wide range. She appeared more than two hundred times at the Met until 1919, when she abruptly quit, thereafter making a career of concert recitals.

Sieglinde today, was his pupil. She seldom made a move professionally without him."

"Semple? What do you know about her?"

"She's a dramatic soprano from Trenton. Salz heard her sing a couple of years ago when she was broke and could not afford to pay for lessons. He took her on, worked with her, coached her, and finally brought her up from obscurity. He had her under some kind of contract."

"Where was Miss Semple when he died?"

"On stage. Sleeping."

Quentin lifted an inquiring eyebrow.

"It's in the score," Van Cleff explained. "You see, in the second act, when Wotan—"

Quentin cut it short. "Some other time." He indicated the pint bottle of whiskey resting on the desk. "Ever see that before?"

"Not until they took it from Salz's pocket."

"Was the man a heavy drinker?"

Van Cleff shrugged. "Rudolf Salz had a lot to forget. Liquor helped."

"Yeah." Quentin, recognizing the usual rationalization, dismissed it carelessly. He said, "Salz probably ducked his head for a snifter and that was the last drink he ever took." His gaze went up as the door opened.

Detective-Sergeant Cullen poked his head in. "There's a bird out here named Stark. Claims he knows something about the bottle."

Quentin glanced at Van Cleff, who said, "That would be Howard Stark, Elsa Vaughn's business manager."

"Send him in."

Cullen threw the door open and a man advanced energetically into the room. He was above medium height, well built, with a little brushwork of silver at his temples, and wore heavy shell glasses on a scholarly face. He was obviously laboring under a strain, and he stopped short when he saw Van Cleff.

"You have some information?" Quentin said.

"For you alone."

Van Cleff took the hint. "I'll be available when you need me, Lieutenant."

When the door closed behind him, Stark moved up to the desk and fixed his eyes on the bottle of scotch. There was a hint of sweat on his forehead. His fists were tightly clenched. He swallowed hard and looked at the Lieutenant.

Quentin prompted him: "You recognize that bottle?"

"Yes, sir." He gulped. "It's the one I bought for Miss Vaughn this morning. I—how did Salz get it?"

Quentin sat erect. The situation had become explosive. He had heard of Elsa Vaughn and he didn't like the idea of a famous opera star being involved in a murder case.

"That scotch is a standard brand," he said. "How do you know it's the same bottle?"

"By that small label. I bought it in Rockville Center this morning and the salesman pasted one of the store's labels on it. Besides, I checked Miss Vaughn's dressing room. The bottle I left there is missing."

Quentin looked at him. "Does Miss Vaughn usually drink scotch during a performance?"

"Of course not." Stark was aggrieved. "A drop of sherry occasionally, that's all. Everyone knows that."

"Then why the scotch?"

"Because a couple of reporters were coming in after the performance. Dave Lang had arranged an interview."

"Who is Dave Lang?"

"Miss Vaughn's publicity man. She is a sports enthusiast. She just bought a large share of a professional football team and the reporters were going to do a piece on it."*

Quentin was thoughtfully chewing the inside of his cheek. He finally broke the silence. "Okay, that's settled. Salz got hold of Miss Vaughn's liquor. The point is, who disliked Salz enough to poison it?"

"That's just it." Stark ran his fingers agitatedly through his hair. "The poison wound up in the wrong body. I think it was intended for Miss Vaughn."

Quentin's chair scraped back as he landed upright on both feet. *"What?"*

"That's right, Lieutenant. Strange things have been happening around here. For weeks now somebody has been trying to injure Miss Vaughn."

"Cullen!"

The Sergeant opened the door and put his head through. "Yes, sir."

"Get Elsa Vaughn up here. On the double."

When the door closed, Quentin turned back to Howard Stark. His voice had lost its mildness. "What kind of things?" he demanded.

Stark was mopping his forehead with a handkerchief. He looked tired. He pulled up a chair and sat down. "It started about

---

* In 1950, when the story likely takes place, professional football was not the predominant American sport that it is today, and team revenues were largely derived from ticket sales. Football suffered badly during World War II, with the loss of players and a decline in attendance. Television was not yet a significant source of revenue, as only a few teams televised selected games. The first nationally televised National Football League championship game did not occur until 1951. In 1949, the Philadelphia Eagles team was sold for $250,000 (about $5 million in 2021's inflated dollars; Samuel H. Williamson, "Purchasing Power Today of a US Dollar Transaction in the Past," Measuring Worth, 2021, http://www.measuringworth.com), a high for the sport but a pittance compared to 2021's valuations, when, for example, the Dallas Cowboys are estimated to be worth in excess of $6 billion. Famously, Helen Traubel herself owned a share of the St. Louis Browns baseball team.

three weeks ago. Miss Vaughn had just opened a brand-new jar of cold cream and was about to apply it when some sixth sense rang a warning bell. The cream was filled with ground glass. Two weeks ago, a huge piece of scenery toppled over as she passed, missed her by a matter of inches. The other night, just before a performance, she found a vase of gladiolas on her dressing room table. Nobody knows where they came from. Miss Vaughn suffers from hay fever, and someone had extracted the pollen from ragweed and scattered the dust over the gladiolas. Miss Vaughn had a mild attack and had to cancel out." Stark pinched out a humorless smile. "A sneeze during Brünnehilde's battle cry could have ruined the performance."

"Who took her place?"

"Hilda Semple."

"Any feud exist between those two?"

"Well…not exactly." Stark looked ill at ease. "I don't like to make accusations, especially without proof, but Semple is a very ambitious woman. Taking top honors at the Met is an obsession with her. But she'll never get there so long as Miss Vaughn is alive and she knows it."

"Do you think she had anything to do with those attempts against Miss Vaughn?"

Stark shrugged, as the door opened and Cullen ushered Elsa Vaughn into the room.

While her business manager performed the amenities, Quentin appraised her. He saw a tall woman constructed in the liberal proportions of the most Wagnerian sopranos. Her carriage was erect and stately, and she met his gaze with candid eyes and a tentative but friendly smile. Her manner was unassuming and she seemed free from the temperament generally associated with prima donnas. At the moment, however, her face still bore traces of the recent ordeal.

Elsa, on her part, was favorably impressed by the Lieutenant's quiet air of authority. He said, "Sit down, Miss Vaughn. Mr. Stark has just told me about a number of attempts to put a halt to your career."

She shot a glance of reproof at her manager. "I thought we were going to keep it a secret, Howard."

"I'm sorry, Elsa." His tone was dogged. "We can't afford to play tag with this thing any longer. It's wide open now. Somebody has stopped fooling and means business. The poison that killed Salz was in that bottle." He aimed a finger at the desk. "The one I brought you for the interview. And I think the poison was meant for you, too."

Elsa looked at him blankly.

Stark swallowed and plunged on. "Rudolf Salz was murdered by mistake and that means only one thing. You're not out of danger. The killer will try again."

The sentence seemed to echo in the room. Then Elsa found her voice and whispered, "I can't believe it—"

"Sounds incredible, doesn't it?" Stark was brusque. "But I'm a businessman, Elsa. I believe in facts. And the facts are clear."

Quentin backed him up. "He's right, Miss Vaughn. I'd like to know why the police weren't notified."

"You can blame me for that," Stark said. "It was the kind of publicity I hoped to avoid."

"Couldn't this Dave Lang you mentioned handle it with discretion?"

"No, sir. That's not the way he operates."

"Now, Howard," Elsa said, "we're living in the twentieth century, competing with all sorts of—"

"I've heard that argument before. It's Dave Lang's, not yours. You're an opera star, not a circus clown or a flagpole sitter."*

---

* Traubel did not limit herself to opera; she also appeared regularly in nightclubs and on television and in films, often in comedic settings poking fun at herself and the "seriousness" of opera.

Quentin raised a hand. "Let's table it for now," he said shortly. There was obviously friction here—a situation worth exploring. But it would have to wait. He shook his head. "I can't understand you people. You pay taxes to hire the best police department in the world and then completely ignore it. Now look at the results. Rudolf Salz is dead, and it could easily have been you, Miss Vaughn."

"But Dave Lang was investigating."

"With what qualifications?"

"He was an O.S.S. officer during the war,"* Stark said. "He fancies himself as an amateur detective."

Quentin made a hopeless gesture. "Okay. We'll get to him later." He turned toward Elsa. "About those attacks, Miss Vaughn. Any idea who was behind them?"

She shook her head.

"Mr. Stark here nominates Hilda Semple."

Elsa moved uncomfortably. "I don't know. Maybe I have too much faith in people. I just can't believe that Hilda would actually attempt anything so..." The rest of it died on her lips.

Quentin was patient. "Let's examine it. I understand Rudolf Salz was her teacher, that she was studying all your roles, that in all probability she would step into your shoes if anything happened. Is that true?"

"I—well, yes."

"Do you have any enemies outside the opera?"

"No, Lieutenant. Not one."

"Then these attacks must be due to your position here. Would they stop if you left the Met?"

---

* The Office of Strategic Services was created in 1942 by President Franklin D. Roosevelt to coordinate wartime intelligence activities. The agency was officially terminated in 1945 but was replaced by the Central Intelligence Agency, which essentially assumed most of its functions.

"Certainly." It was Stark who answered and he did so with conviction. "But naturally, that's out of the question. She has her commitments."

Quentin raised an eyebrow at him. "Do they pay so liberally?"

"No, sir, they do not. Miss Vaughn commands top prices, but it's still only a drop in the bucket. A single radio engagement is far more remunerative."

Elsa sighed. "That's the businessman talking. There's more to it than that, Lieutenant. I didn't spend the best years of my life studying music just for the money. The Met is a singer's ultimate goal. The satisfaction is enormous."

It was an interesting sidelight, but not what Quentin was after at the moment. "Are you friendly with Hilda Semple?"

"We get along," Elsa said noncommittally.

"How about the others—Van Cleff, for example?"

"Van Cleff's hands are tied," Stark put in. "It's Mrs. DeBrett who fouls up the machinery."

"DeBrett?" Quentin frowned. The name seemed to ring a bell in his memory.

"Edwina DeBrett," Elsa explained. "Patron of the arts. The wife of one of the largest contributors to the Metropolitan Opera Company who is also a member of the board. Power behind the throne."

"Sounds like politics."

"It is." Elsa shrugged wearily. "An opera house is divided by more political factions than the French Chamber of Deputies. One really needs an extra pair of eyes in the back of his head."

"Miss Vaughn is safe," Stark said. "She manages to keep aloof from all politics and intrigue."

"Any idea how Salz could have gotten that bottle out of your room, Miss Vaughn?" Quentin asked.

She shook her head. "None at all."

"Were you on good terms with him?"

She hesitated. "Not lately."

He waited for her to continue.

"We had—well, differences of opinion."

"Would you please elaborate?"

She took a long breath. "I had heard of Salz before he came to this country, and I'd been impressed by his reputation. When he started coaching Wagnerian roles I did some work with him. In this profession one never finishes studying. Rudolf was a painstaking teacher. He had his own methods. He would record my voice on a machine and listen endlessly for errors in phrasing and pronunciation. But there was too much friction between us. We couldn't see eye to eye on a number of things. He was a fanatic on tradition. Any attempt at originality would drive him into a temper. He had sung with many of the great singers in Europe— Gadski, Matzenauer, Nordica, Schumann-Heink.* Every gesture, every step, every nuance, had to conform to his memory of their performances. He even had some old scores with stage directions marked on them. He wanted me to follow them rigidly; I just couldn't see it. An artist must stand on her own interpretation, or be nothing more than a parrot. I wanted latitude, and we had some monumental arguments. Finally, our relations deteriorated completely and we had to give up working together."

"How did Salz take it?"

"Bitterly," Howard Stark said. "He was a vindictive man. I wouldn't be surprised if he was behind those attacks on Miss Vaughn."

Quentin glanced at him. "A little while ago, Hilda Semple seemed to be your candidate."

---

* These are all women who performed over the years at the Met: The celebrated German soprano Johanna Emilia Agnes Gadski (1872–1932); Margaret Matzenauer (1881–1963), a well-known Hungarian mezzo-soprano of Jewish descent; Lillian Nordica (1857–1914), a highly regarded American-born dramatic soprano who was also a model for Coca-Cola; and Ernestine Schumann-Heink (1861–1936), an Austrian-born German-American contralto noted for her wide range.

Stark leaned forward. "But there really isn't much difference, Lieutenant. Between those two there was an identity of interests. She was tied to Salz by contract. He stood to gain through her advancement."

Quentin shook his head. "If that poison was earmarked for Miss Vaughn, then Salz is out. He wouldn't pollute the liquor, then steal it and drink it himself. It had to be someone else."

Stark nodded reluctantly.

"Which means," Quentin added soberly, "that Miss Vaughn is still in danger. A mistake in victims doesn't erase the motive. Our killer will strike again."

Elsa swallowed with an audible gulp.

"You'll have to protect her," Stark said grimly.

"We will, to the best of our ability. But we cannot assign detectives and food tasters to follow every move she makes. I have a suggestion." He looked at her. "It's up to Miss Vaughn. Suppose we keep the plot against you under our hats. We know the score. We can proceed on the assumption that the killer's plans misfired. That puts us one up on him. He'll think we've been misled. Our apparent innocence may influence his future behavior. Since we know what to look for, we can plan accordingly."

"I don't like it." Stark was emphatic. "It's too dangerous."

"She's in danger anyway."

Elsa said, "I'm willing. Unless we do something soon, I'm likely to wind up a nervous wreck."

"Good." Quentin was pleased. "I'll take the necessary steps." He stood up. "Where can I find this Dave Lang?"

"He must be around somewhere," Elsa said. "He was supposed to meet us backstage with those reporters after the opera."

The Lieutenant went to the door and spoke to Sergeant Cullen. "A publicity man named Dave Lang. Find him."

CHAPTER THREE

Good tenors are always scarce. But a dramatic tenor, with the necessary physique, capable of standing up under the taxing roles of Wagner, is a rare and valuable commodity.

In his first season at the Met, Karl Ecker was building an enviable reputation. Swart of complexion, and with a clean-boned, handsome face, he had the great barrel chest of a true *Heldentenor*. An awareness of his considerable talents was reflected in his manner, a strange amalgam of geniality and arrogance. He could be warm and intimate at one moment, distant and cold in the next.

He was angry at Rudolf Salz. The man's death in the prompter's box had been an unforgettable sight. It had affected his performance and that was one thing he could never forgive. Salz should have died elsewhere.

Now, at the end of the opera, Ecker proceeded at once to his dressing room on the Thirty-ninth Street side of the building. He halted in front of the door. Someone was playing the small upright piano in his dressing room. Strains of the "Liebestod" came through.* There was an almost imperceptible tightening of the skin around his eyes and mouth, then he opened the door and stepped in. A woman, seated at the piano, turned and looked up.

"Hello, Edwina," he said quietly.

The music had not relaxed her face, and a wonderfully preserved face it was considering that she had used it for nearly four decades. Ebony hair was arranged in an elaborate coiffure. Her eyes were gray, tilted and feline. Everything about Edwina DeBrett was feline, even her movements as she rose to greet him, a half smile on her cyclamen-red lips.†

"Where were you last night, Karl?" Her voice was a purr.

"Had a headache, *Liebchen.*" He closed his eyes and pressed his temples between two fingertips.

"I think you are lying." She had not raised her voice.

"Am I?"

"Yes. I phoned your apartment several times. There was no answer." She looked at him reproachfully. "I gave that reception especially for you, Karl. You were the guest of honor. Your failure to appear made me look rather silly."

He turned toward the mirror. "Shall I explain again, *Liebchen*? I do not like receptions. I do not like society matrons fawning over me. Nor do I like domestic complications, especially the way Stanley has been staring at me lately."

"Don't worry about my husband."

"Somebody has to worry about him."

---

* Literally, "Love death," this is one of the most famous excerpts from Wagnerian opera—the final dramatic scene from his *Tristan und Isolde* (first performed in 1865), as Isolde sings over the body of her deceased love, Tristan. The "Liebestod" is often played in other contexts to foreshadow doomed love.

---

† Cyclamen is a species of flowering plant, and it grows in many varieties and shades of red. In 1947, the House of Houbigant company marketed a "Translucid Deep Cyclamen" shade of lipstick that it described as "tropical red."

"I can handle Stanley."

He shrugged, sat down at the table, and reached for a bottle of alcohol to dissolve the spirit gum that held his wig on. He patted this on with a wad of absorbent cotton and then began to pluck out the tufts of hair which made up his sideburns.

"I'm afraid, *Liebchen*," he said casually, "that you have a tendency to underestimate Stanley. I know your husband quite well. I was once married to his sister, remember? He did not become a successful capitalist by reason of some mental deficiency. Besides, we must keep him in good humor. The opera needs money and Stanley controls the purse strings. We ought not to see each other so frequently."

"You had no such scruples a couple of months ago. Why this sudden concern?"

"An attack of conscience, Edwina." He winced as the last remnant of hair came away from his cheek, and winced again when she purred a name at him. "Now, Edwina," he said, "that's hardly the kind of talk for the wife of a board member."

"You might remember, Karl, that it was my influence that got you into the Met."

"It was your influence that got me an audition," he corrected her, "but it was my talent that got me the contract. And it is my ability that will keep me here." He reached for a jar of cold cream.

"It means a lot to you, singing at the Met, doesn't it Karl?"

He caught the curious inflection in her voice and spun around, his expression stony. "Yes, Edwina, it means a lot to me. It means everything. The Met has always been my goal."

Her voice continued to purr. "Tell me, Karl, was I merely a rung in the ladder? Were you being nice to me because I could help?"

He laughed shortly. "Nonsense."

"Because if I thought that..."

"Then what, Edwina? Your hands are tied."

"Are they, Karl? Do you remember what happened to LaSalle, the baritone?" He frowned, and she went on. "Such a little scandal. Only a few stones smuggled in from Holland among his costumes. A fine and a suspended sentence. But what damage to his reputation! Wasn't it sad, Karl, how the Met dropped him instantly? Of course you remember, Karl. LaSalle is still singing in beer halls."

"My past is clear."

"Don't be so sure."

He stood up, towering over her. "What do you mean?"

"Nothing. Nothing at all, Karl darling. Shall we be friends?"

His face changed. Suddenly he smiled, a dazzling transformation. His arms opened and she came toward him. Their kiss was intense, but almost at once Karl moved back.

"We must be careful, *Liebchen*," he said. "Somebody may walk in. Police are all over the place."

Thick brows descended in a frown over his eyes. "How did you manage to get backstage anyway? I thought all the doors were blocked."

"I've been here all along, up in Van Cleff's office. I—" She stopped as a knock sounded on the door.

Ecker looked up. "Yes?"

Sergeant Cullen poked his head into the room. "Lieutenant Quentin wants everybody up in the anteroom, without delay, please."

CHAPTER FOUR

Dave Lang was attractive, under thirty, radiating good will. Crew-cut hair and a bow-tie gave him an undergraduate appearance. His movements were quick and dynamic and a bit overwhelming. His boyishness was balanced by eyes that were alert and missed nothing. He breezed into Lieutenant Quentin's presence with his hand outstretched, brash, confident, and exuberant.

"Understand you wanted to see me, Lieutenant. I'm Dave Lang, in charge of Miss Vaughn's publicity. Got half a dozen reporters waiting outside. How about a statement? A murder at the Met! Brother!"

Quentin liberated his hand. "Later. Sit down, please."

Lang sat.

"A lot of people are waiting to be interviewed, Mr. Lang. Important people. I'd like to clear them through as soon as possible. But I'm talking to you first, so we'll cut out the preliminaries. I've already spoken to Miss Vaughn. I know about those attacks directed against her. She tells me you were doing some spadework on it. All right. Let's have your report."

Lang became serious. He spoke crisply. "There isn't any,

Lieutenant. My batting average is zero. I couldn't turn up the smallest fragment of information. These musicians are a queer lot. It's hard to get a straight answer. And if they suspect anyone of prying into their affairs they button up tight."

"Miss Vaughn seems normal enough."

"They all do, but they're absolutely unpredictable. I don't know—maybe Miss Vaughn is an exception."

"Do you think some member of the company is responsible?"

"Probably. An outsider would lack freedom of movement backstage."

Quentin said, "These attacks are serious. There was a lot at stake. How come you undertook the job?"

"It was Miss Vaughn's idea, not mine. She was trying to avoid unpleasant publicity. She felt that as part of her normal entourage, I could move around without suspicion. Protective coloration, sort of. That way I might catch someone off guard and pick up a clue. But it didn't work. I found myself up against a very cagey individual."

"Dig in, sir. Have you any ideas?"

Dave shook his head. "Afraid not."

"Her business manager suggested Hilda Semple."

"I know. And I kept an eye on her."

"Well?"

"Nothing, except..."

"Open up," Quentin said. "Let's have it."

"Well"—Lang was reluctant—"she—er—was having a thing with that tenor, Karl Ecker."

Quentin waved it impatiently away. The romantic proclivities of these people might bear scrutiny later, but murder was the important item now. His eyes were calculating, weighing the man before him. He came to a swift decision.

"Stark also suggested Rudolf Salz," he said.

Dave Lang frowned. "How come?"

"Because of a contract between them. Salz owned a piece of Semple's career. He stood to gain by her advancement."

Lang turned his palms up. "If Salz was behind those attacks, then Miss Vaughn is safe. He's out of the picture now."

Quentin shook his head. "You're wrong. Salz is out, but Miss Vaughn is still in danger. The poison that killed Salz came out of a liquor bottle that was in her dressing room."

Dave Lang jumped to his feet. "Good Lord! Then Salz must have been killed by mistake."

"Exactly. Howard Stark bought that bottle and left it in her dressing room. How Salz managed to get hold of it, we don't know. I'm telling you this so you'll know the score. It's not for publication, understand? Keep it under your hat."

Lang collapsed weakly into his chair. He kept shaking his head from side to side and his voice was awed. "I knew somebody was trying to break up her career, but I never thought it would go as far as murder."

"It has." Quentin was grim. "But we've got to cover all angles. It's possible that Salz was actually the intended victim. Which means we'll have to put his past under a microscope. In observing Hilda Semple, did you pick up any information about the man at all? Anything, no matter how trivial, may be of use."

Dave pondered, eyebrows pulled together. "Sorry, Lieutenant, I wasn't concentrating on Salz. All I know is that he had only two students left, Hilda Semple and Karl Ecker."

Quentin rose and moved to the window. He looked out for a prolonged moment and then turned. "I've seen some beauts in the last few years, but this one takes the cake. Time, place, and execution. The Metropolitan Opera House in the middle of a performance. What a field day the newspapers are going to have! And a lot of big shots will begin to pull strings. 'Take it easy,

Lieutenant. The soft pedal here. These people are sensitive.'" He took a snorting breath. "People! Hell, they're not people; they're musicians!"

Lang nodded in sympathy. "I know just what you mean, Lieutenant."

"Do you?"

"Yes, sir. Music appeals to the emotions more than the intelligence. These people live highly emotional lives. You never can tell what one of them is liable to do next." He frowned. "Wasn't one of them involved in some kind of case last year? Karl Ecker, I believe."

Quentin said, "The papers were full of it. Where were you?"

"On the coast at the time. It reached us only vaguely. If you'd brief me on it, maybe I can help. I've got a few pipelines into the musical world."

Quentin glanced at his watch. A few minutes more or less wouldn't hurt; the others could wait. He knew how to relate a story, keeping the facts unvarnished.

He said, "Two years ago, Karl Ecker was unknown and practically broke. Then he met Ivy DeBrett and married her."

"Any relation to Stanley DeBrett, the financier?"

"His sister."

"You know, I suppose, that Stanley's wife, Edwina DeBrett, is one of the big wheels here at the Met."

"Yes. No more interruptions, please. Let me get on with it. At the time, some people said that Ecker married Ivy for her money. I wouldn't know. At any rate, he didn't let it stand in his way. And they had something in common: love for music. She wanted to be a singer herself. It was an obsession. Only, she had no voice. The marriage gave Ecker's career a push. He was engaged for a few concerts and began to make a reputation for himself.

"Then, a year ago last winter, he was scheduled for an

appearance in Philadelphia. Ivy usually went with him, but this time she had a cold. Ecker arrived there with his accompanist, and spent the afternoon resting and rehearsing. At eight-thirty he entered the hall. That was February fifth. You weren't here, so you wouldn't remember. Worst blizzard since '88.* Ten inches of snow. Rail lines tied up, planes grounded, no transportation of any kind. Ecker was forced to stay over in Philadelphia. At noon the next day, he arrived home. Ivy was dead. He found her on the living-room floor with a bullet hole through her temple."

Dave Lang sat motionless, eyes intent. For a moment, the office was very quiet.

"The apartment was a shambles," Quentin went on. "Evidently there had been a struggle. Ivy's jewelry was missing. Family heirlooms and antiques, valuable stuff. It went down in the books as armed robbery."

"And the gun?" Dave asked.

"No trace of it. A thirty-two, according to the bullet. She'd been shot at contact. There were no powder burns around the wound."

"And the case?"

"Still unsolved." Quentin's mouth was bleak.

"Who inherited Ivy's money?"

"Ecker—what was left of it."

Dave frowned. "What do you mean?"

"Bad investments. During the last year her estate had dwindled to almost nothing. However, there was an insurance policy which Ecker collected. It paid double indemnity. Fifty grand."

"That's nothing to sneeze at." Dave pursed his lips. "People

---

* There was a severe blizzard in Philadelphia in 1888 and again in 1899. More than ten inches of snow fell in Philadelphia in 1941 but not again until 1960. The last severe Northeastern blizzard before 1951 (when *Metropolitan Opera Murders* was published) occurred in December 1947. Therefore, either the city of Ecker's performance or the blizzard itself must be regarded as fictional.

have been killed for less. Couldn't he have made the trip, storm or no storm, and then doubled back in a matter of hours?"

"Not a chance." Quentin's tone was decided. "Whenever a woman is killed, our first suspect is always the husband. We checked him up, down, and sideways. Ecker stayed in Philadelphia all night."

"Who says so?"

"His accompanist. There was a convention in town and the hotels were jammed. They had to share a room and the accompanist stayed with him all night."

"Sure, and a couple of sleeping pills could have stored the accompanist away in mothballs."

"We went into that. It's our business to think of everything. The man had insomnia. He sat up all night, composing a fugue, whatever that is. He swore that Ecker slept right through till morning."

"No chance of collusion?"

"There's always a chance of collusion where money is involved. But a cop often works on instinct, Lang, and that boy was telling the truth. I'll stake my reputation on it. What's more, Ecker had over thirty-two hundred witnesses to prove his alibi."

Dave gaped at him. "Huh?"

"That's right. Thirty-two hundred witnesses. Ivy was killed between nine and ten P.M., as established and confirmed by the Medical Examiner. At that precise hour, Karl Ecker was singing a program of German lieder* before an auditorium full of people."

Dave was finally sold. "And what," he asked, "was Ecker's reaction?"

"He became violently ill. The slug had torn a hole through

---

* Literally, songs—usually referring to the German art song tradition of the Classical and Romantic eras. Franz Schubert, Robert Schumann, Ludwig van Beethoven, Wolfgang Amadeus Mozart, and others frequently set poetry to music.

her beam and she was not a pretty sight. He finally managed to get through to Headquarters and I was on the scene in fifteen minutes."

"No sign of forcible entry?"

Quentin shook his head. "None. However, she might have answered the bell and even admitted her assailant. He could have been someone she knew, or someone who had a key."

The door opened wide enough to admit Sergeant Cullen. "Got them all collected now, Lieutenant," he said. "They're a handful, all right, especially that Hilda Semple. I think you'd better…"

He was cut short by a minor typhoon in the person of a large blonde woman who projected herself unceremoniously into the room. She advanced grimly, stopped short of the desk, and glared at Quentin with eyes that were both scrappy and indignant. Her hands were on her hips and her mouth was compressed into a thin line of exasperation.

"Are you the man in charge? I'm Hilda Semple. I've been standing in that anteroom for over an hour arguing with your subordinates. It's getting late and I've been here since noon. I have a dinner engagement and I'm hungry. I'd like to leave at once. Would you please issue instructions?"

Quentin held himself under control, but his manner was noticeably lacking in warmth. "Your dinner will have to wait, Miss Semple. A man has been killed."

"I know," she said shortly. "But I didn't kill him and I don't see where it's any affair of mine."

Quentin glanced wearily at Dave Lang. "I'll want to see you later. Stay on tap."

Both Lang and Sergeant Cullen departed. When the door had closed behind them, Quentin waved at a chair. "Sit down, Miss Semple."

"I'd prefer to stand."

"As you wish." He was appraising her openly. Wagnerian sopra-nos, apparently, were all poured from a single mold: of Amazonian stature, deeply bosomed, with lungs and diaphragm equipped to meet the most uncompromising demands. Her hair, he noted, was of a shade similar to Elsa Vaughn's. There, however, the resem-blance ended. There was about this woman, despite her present anger, a sort of stolid inscrutability. He felt, instinctively, that her emotions were limited.

Quentin was a diplomat. He managed a diplomatic smile. "Since you're in such a hurry, I'll take you now, Miss Semple. You'll have to answer a few questions."

"I'm ready. But please be brief."

His smile was under a strain. "You knew Rudolf Salz rather well."

"He was my teacher."

"I understand you were on stage when he died."

"Yes, but I saw nothing. I was singing the role of Sieglinde, who was supposed to be sleeping at the time."

"Then you did not see him take the fatal drink?"

"My eyes were closed."

Quentin regarded her curiously. The death of Salz hadn't touched her at all. She seemed oddly unaffected. It was peculiar, and he hold her so bluntly.

"For a person who was closely associated with the deceased, Miss Semple, I find your attitude strangely unconcerned."

"That's quite true, Lieutenant. I'll make a confession. I didn't like Rudolf Salz very much. He was not a nice person."

"Then why didn't you break off and leave him?"

"Because he was still the best teacher available."

"Is that the only reason?" He was watching her closely.

"What other reason could there be?"

"Your contract with him."

She became suddenly wary. Whatever expression was on her face retired behind an impersonal mask. She stared at him coldly through an interval of silence. Then she said, "I'm sorry, Lieutenant. I can't discuss the matter. You'll have to talk it over with my lawyer."

Quentin smiled inwardly. He had pushed the right button.

"Was your lawyer here when Salz was killed?"

"No, of course not."

"Then I can't see where he'd be any help. I'd like to point out one thing, Miss Semple: whatever we have to know we can find out. Stubbornness will gain you nothing. It might pay to co-operate with us."

She stood quietly, considering. "What is it you want, Lieutenant?"

"Information about your contract. You may as well talk. We'll probably find a copy in Salz's safe-deposit box."

"All right. It called for fifty per cent of my earnings." She smiled thinly at Quentin's look of surprise. "Sounds excessive, doesn't it? Well, it is. It's unspeakably outrageous. The man was a bloodsucker."

"You signed it," he said logically. "No one stood over you with a gun."

"Quite true. But I had no choice. There are other methods of coercion besides the use of a gun."

"Such as?"

"When I first met Rudolf Salz, I was working in a department store. The salary was hardly generous. Certainly not enough to pay for singing lessons." An odd intensity entered her voice. "Do you know what frustration is, Lieutenant? To have a talent that keeps clawing and scratching inside of you to be developed? That keeps you restless and nervous and constantly on edge? It's not easy. And then, one day, I met Rudolf Salz. He heard me sing. He liked my voice. He felt it had great possibilities, and he made me an offer. He would teach me to sing, and when I knew how to use my voice properly, he would coach me in all the Wagnerian roles. On a contingent basis. There would be no fee. He would receive fifty per cent of everything I earned for a period of ten years."

"And he's been collecting ever since?"

"Yes."

"He knew you were dissatisfied?"

"I made no secret of it." She took a long breath. "As a matter of fact, I had consulted my lawyer. He told me the contract was binding. Nevertheless we were going to start a lawsuit anyway in an attempt to modify it."

"Salz was aware of this?"

"Yes." Her smile was brittle. "I know what you're thinking, Lieutenant. That maybe I killed Rudolf Salz to end the contract. It's not true."

He was rubbing a thumb knuckle across the angle of his jaw, considering, his eyes half closed. At last he broke the silence. "Thank you, Miss Semple. If I need anything else, I'll get in touch with you."

"I may leave now?"

He gave an affirmative nod. When she opened the door to go, an irritated babble of voices came through. He inhaled deeply, straightened his shoulders, and went out to face the assembled musicians. He carried himself with the resigned but determined air of a Christian martyr entering the arena.

CHAPTER FIVE

It is amazing what twenty-four hours can do. The passage of time, even one day, had dissolved most of the shock and horror which had accompanied the violent passing of Rudolf Salz. Elsa Vaughn, seated at her Baldwin,* had managed to forget it for minutes at a time. Venetian blinds, tilted against the huge studio windows, allowed just the proper amount of sunlight to fall upon her fingers as they skipped agilely over the keys.

She was not alone. In the curve of the piano stood a young girl, slim and straight, her fingertips peaked together in the classic pose of a singer. From the oval formed by her lips came a light lyric voice, running up the scale. The seriousness of her face was softened by a rather wistful expression around the eyes. Her jaw, however, was small, pointed, and determined. The over-all effect, examined from any angle, was more than pleasant.

Reaching the top of the scale, her voice wavered and was abruptly punctuated by a thundering chord on the piano.

"No, no," Elsa said. "You're still choking the high ones. Let them flow, Jane dear, round and smooth."

---

* A popular brand of piano.

She made a high, upward gesture and demonstrated, head back, suspending a high note on the still air, holding it, her face relaxed and smiling. "See what I mean? Come now, let's try again."

As Elsa's protégée, Jane DeBrett took her singing lesson with earnest gravity. Brown hair fell softly about her face. Her figure was lissome and athletic. Her voice, lacking volume, had yet an appealing quality, which she handled effortlessly and with considerable charm. While her father, Stanley DeBrett, could easily afford to pay for her lessons, he had so far exhibited a notable lack of enthusiasm toward a musical career for his only daughter. In Elsa, an old friend, she had found a sympathetic ally.

She came here several times a week. She liked Elsa's studio. It was warm and comfortable. The furniture was built to accommodate any of the heroic figures conceived by their favorite composer, Richard Wagner. Against the far wall there was a small bar with an assortment of beverages. Above it, in a simple frame, hung an original Degas.* And near the piano Elsa kept a recording machine capable of capturing the whole audio range. Its purchase had been suggested originally by Rudolf Salz.

Jane held her top note with assurance and then cut it off as her breath ran low. Elsa swung away from the piano, nodding with approval.

"Much better, darling. Anyone could see the improvement."

Jane was pleased. Elsa's praise was never given lightly.

"Do you think I'm ready for my concert?"

---

* Oil paintings of French Impressionist Edgar Degas and his contemporaries, such as Paul Gauguin, sold for prices in the high five-figure, low six-figure range in the 1940s and 1950s; today, they sell for two to three hundred times as much. Unsigned pastels were available then for much more modest prices, and signed pastels and drawings are still sold for only tens of thousands. Miss Vaughn, who could afford to buy a "large share of a professional football team," for what was presumably a six-figure amount (see note on page 10), may well have purchased a Degas oil for herself.

"Almost. You know, Jane, I've been thinking. We should add another aria to your program."

"Whatever you say, Elsa."

"'Un Bel Di, Vedremo.' You do it so well."

"Let's try it now, shall we?"

Elsa swung back to the piano and began to play. Jane's voice was admirably suited to this haunting melody from *Madama Butterfly*, which descends so curiously from a high G flat. There were feeling and style in her rendition. As the last note died, Elsa applauded and said, "Bravo."

Jane came around and sat beside her on the stool "Oh, Elsa, I've made so much progress! How can I ever thank you?"

"By continuing to love music."

"Will I ever be famous?"

Elsa studied her carefully. "Is that what you really want, my dear?"

"More than anything in this world." There was intensity in her voice, almost fierceness. "I—I don't want to be just a rich man's daughter. I want to do something for myself. I want to be somebody. I want someday to stand on one of the great stages of the world and feel that I am holding an audience spellbound."

Elsa waited a moment, then said softly, "Tell me, darling, are you sure you're not just trying to prove something to your stepmother?"

Jane stiffened slightly, her forehead ridged. "I don't understand."

Elsa leaned toward her, serious. "All this burning ambition of yours—isn't it due to Edwina's amused tolerance, treating your desire to sing as though she were humoring a child?"

---

* This magnificent aria is from Act II of Giacomo Puccini's tragic *Madama Butterfly*, first performed in 1904. In it, the courtesan Butterfly imagines that "One fine day, we'll see…" her lover Lieutenant Pinkerton returning to her. It remains one of the most popular arias for sopranos.

Jane bit her lip and was silent for a moment, her eyes lowered. "That may be part of it," she admitted reluctantly. "But only a small part. You know how I feel about Edwina. I'd like to make her swallow her opinion."

"Come now, Jane. You needn't worry about Edwina's opinions. They're not very reliable."

"I know. I've heard her express them too often. She thinks Hilda Semple is the greatest thing since Schumann-Heink. She says her range is enormous."

Elsa said, "I have a bigger range in my kitchen."

It broke the tension and they both laughed.

Elsa sighed. "God help the Met if Van Cleff had to abide by all of Edwina's artistic decisions. Do me a favor, will you, Jane? Forget Edwina. Forget her attitudes about your music. You mustn't let trivial emotional factors of that sort influence important decisions in your life. You like to sing, you want to sing, then do so. But let me give you some advice, and it comes from years of experience, believe me. There are other things equally important as a career, perhaps more so. You want to give a concert at Town Hall. Okay. Howard is arranging it for you. It's a small triumph, I know. But try to be satisfied with it and polish your repertoire."

"No." Jane's voice was firm, her mouth obstinate, her jaw set. Both fists were tightly clenched in her lap. "My goal is the opera. And I don't want to sing any fancy Italian operas. I want to sing Wagner—with you."

Elsa appealed heavenward. "She wants to sing Wagner. No, darling, I'm afraid not. Your voice is too small."

"It can be developed. I do all the exercises you tell me."

"But it's not only your voice, darling. It's you. Your figure, your physical resources. You could never stand up under a regimen of German opera. You'd need more strength. Would you be willing to gain a hundred pounds?"

"Yes—if it would help my voice."

Elsa threw up her hands in utter defeat. "Everything for art, eh? My God, darling, you're young. You're beautiful. Count your blessings, and consider the romantic aspects. Men today prefer their women small and trim. Nobody falls in love with a two-hundred-pound soprano."

"Is love so important, Elsa?"

"Important? Empires have been wrecked because of love. And where would the human race be without it?"

"But you never got married."

"That's true. And I'll be the first to admit that I may have missed something. I'm no longer sure that I did the wise thing in giving up everything for a career."

"Did you have to?"

"At first, yes. There isn't time for anything else. Do you know how much work is involved in learning just one new opera? The endless hours spent in studying the score, going over it again and again, until you can visualize in your mind the relationship between words and music, until the psychology and emotions of the characters become a part of your own being, so that you can project yourself into the story as though it were all really happening. How the music and text must percolate through your bloodstream, so that they become fused as one and the tempi fixed in your mind. How unceasingly you must work to perfect your breath control to ensure the proper melodic variations. And the long, arduous hours one must spend mastering foreign tongues. No, Jane, it never ends. And all that work for only one opera. And to amount to anything you must learn many."

Jane, listening with rapt attention, gave no indication of wavering in her determination. "But you did all that, Elsa, and you're not sorry now, are you?"

"I did it because I had to. Don't you understand, darling, for years music was my whole life. By taking it away you deprived me of the very air I breathed. But you're different, Jane."

"No, I'm not. Really." Jane shook her head. "I wouldn't mind anything if I could only be sure there was some chance of success."

"That would make life simpler, wouldn't it? But there is no guarantee of success. And even if you could never achieve your ambition, if you could never stand on the stage of a great opera house, I would still tell you to study—for your own pleasure. What's wrong with Puccini, Verdi, Mascagni, Rossini?* They wrote beautiful operas, just suited to your voice. But you mustn't devote your life to them. Look what happened to your aunt—how she suffered because she could never get anywhere."

"Aunt Ivy had no talent."

"That's true, Jane. But talent isn't such a scarce commodity. There are wonderful voices being trained all over the country. They can't all be successful or even hope to reach the Met. If you—"

The doorbell rang. Elsa started to rise. Jane waved her back. "I'll get it," she said, heading through the foyer to reach the door.

When she pulled it open, the young man facing her across the threshold started to smile, staring at her with frank and uninhibited admiration. Warm color began to rise in Jane's cheeks, but she met his gaze squarely. "Yes?" she asked.

He had to clear his throat. "Miss Vaughn, please. Tell her it's Dave Lang."

But Elsa had heard his voice and she called out a welcome.

"Come on in, Dave." She had swung away from the piano and

---

* Of this famous group of nineteenth-century Italian composers of opera, perhaps only Mascagni will not be familiar: Pietro Mascagni (1863–1945) is principally famous for *Cavalleria Rusticana* (1890), which changed the course of Italian opera, the first of the post-Romantic *verismo* (Italian for "realism") movement.

was waiting with her hand outstretched. "Glad you stopped—What's the matter with you, Dave? Haven't you ever seen a girl before? Say hello to Jane DeBrett."

"Hello." He had not taken his eyes off Jane.

"This is my publicity man, Jane. Dave Lang."

Jane acknowledged the introduction with a demure smile.

Elsa's gesture embraced the room. "Sit down, Dave. We'll be free in a moment. I'm giving a lesson."

He made himself inconspicuous on the edge of a chair in the far corner. There was an odd look on his face, as if he had been hypnotized. His pulse beat quicker and his blood seemed warmer and he listened to her sing in a kind of fog. An abrupt thump on the piano keys startled him.

"No," Elsa said. "Look"—she pinched her throat lightly—"the larynx is a delicate musical instrument, Jane. It controls the air that produces sound. Your tone must be floated on the breath so that the softest pianissimo will be heard even in the gallery. Try again."

Jane took a deep breath. A chord set the pitch. Her voice lingered on the still air like the vibration of a clear bell.

"That's it," Elsa said. "Well"—she turned to Dave—"what do you think?"

He let out a fervent breath. "Perfect."

Jane smiled warmly. "Thank you."

Elsa slapped fingertips against her forehead. "I'm slow today. An idea just struck me. If you really like her voice, Dave, we have a job for you. Jane is making her debut next month at Town Hall. She could use a little publicity. It might sell some tickets. What do you say?"

He was on his feet at once. "I'm hired." He came close to the girl. "We'll make this the biggest debut New York ever saw. I'll talk to Winchell.* I'll map out a campaign. A little cheesecake on the cover of *Life* and *Time*. A blurb by Olin Downes.† A word on the air by Deems Taylor.‡ You're liable to have a sellout on your hands, Miss DeBrett. When are you free? We'll talk it over."

"She's free now," Elsa said. "Unless it was something special that brought you here."

He waved it aside. "Nothing of consequence. One of the A.P.§ writers wants to do a feature on that football deal. I merely wanted to set up an interview."

"Any time, Dave. You know my schedule."

"Fine." He turned hopefully to Jane. "A cocktail, Miss DeBrett?"

"Love it." Her eyes were eager.

Five minutes after they had left, Elsa Vaughn was still smiling.

---

* Walter Winchell (1897–1972) was a popular and highly influential gossip columnist and tabloid reporter for newspapers and radio. In the early 1950s, his weekly radio show was also broadcast on television.

---

† Downes (1886–1955) was the music critic for the *New York Times*.

---

‡ Taylor (1885–1966), a critic and a composer himself, was a passionate promoter of classical music. Taylor's operas *The King's Henchman* and *Peter Ibbetson* premiered at the Met in 1927 and 1931, respectively, to great success.

---

§ The Associated Press, founded in 1846, is a cooperative nonprofit news agency and a key disseminator of news reports and news writing to hundreds of its member newspapers and customers. Its principal competitors in 1950 were the United Press International (UPI) and International News Service (INS).

CHAPTER SIX

It was a nice quiet bar on Sixty-third Street, off Madison—a small oasis with wired music, soft lights, and unobtrusive waiters. At this hour most of the booths were vacant. Dave had convoyed Jane through the streets at a leisurely pace, getting acquainted, and now, leaning back against the polished leather, she felt relaxed and peaceful.

When the moon-faced waiter glided over, she gave her order. "A Tahiti Typhoon."* It earned her a look of respect.

Dave said, "I'm an old alcoholic myself, but this is a new one on me. The ingredients, please."

"Cointreau, gin, lime, and a split of champagne," she told him.

He, too, was impressed. "The Langs are a courageous tribe. I'll take the same." And when the waiter was gone, "How many of those can you hold?"

"Not even one. I just like to nurse it along. The flavor entrances me."

"Okay. But I'm willing to bet that two of those in quick succession would turn a coloratura into a baritone."

---

* The origins of the drink are unknown, but it is listed in various classical bar guides dating back to the 1950s and remains popular.

Jane laughed. "A Princeton man I know once drank three of them in a row."

"What happened?"

"They carried him out like an ironing board."

He shook a finger at her. "You're a nice girl, Jane. Stay away from lushes like that. From now on you'd better stick to good, solid citizens."

"Like who, for instance?"

"Me."

She put her head to one side, regarding him quizzically. "I never went out with a publicity man before. Is there any future in it?"

"Sure. A man can live in moderate luxury, and look at all the wonderful people you meet."

"Do you really know Winchell?"

He grinned. "I know Winchell as well as he knows me." The waiter, back with their drinks, set them down and retired discreetly into the shadows. "Kidding aside," Dave said, "all I have to do is send Winchell a hot lead. If he likes it, he'll use it. After all, your father is a well-known financier."

She shook her head. "But I don't want to ride along on Dad's reputation. I want to be a success on my own."

"Naturally. But you need a shove in the right direction. And after this concert you'll be a financier yourself."

She smiled weakly. "I'm afraid not. The last debut that made any money at Town Hall was in '88. People came in to get out of the snow."

"How's that?"

"I thought you knew. Nobody buys tickets at the box office for an unknown singer. Oh, perhaps a few friends or relatives, that's all. In order to get an audience, the house is papered. Unless, of course, people can be lured in with reports of a brilliant new talent."

"Now look," Dave said grimly, "you'll have an audience if I have to drive them in with a bull whip." He paused, frowning. "I still don't get it, though. Why should anyone give a concert that loses money?"

"Any number of reasons, Dave. It's a chance to be heard. There's the fulfillment and satisfaction after years of study. And the opportunity to be reviewed by critics. And how else can one develop stage presence without—"

"Okay. I'm convinced. Finish your drink and I'll buy you another."

She shook her head. "I'm afraid not. Your life wouldn't be worth a farthing rushlight.* Do you know what Dad does to young men who bring me home plastered? He has a shillelagh† that weighs—"

Dave shuddered. "That's enough. Spill it out and I'll get you a lemonade."

They laughed together. Dave sampled his drink and found it potent. He turned the glass in his fingers and admired the highlights burning in Jane's hair. "I didn't know Elsa had a protégée," he said.

"We've been working together for almost a year." Her tone was worshipful. "Elsa's wonderful."

"How did you meet her?"

"She was a friend of my mother's."

"Isn't your mother one of the Board of Directors of the Opera Company?"

"You mean Edwina, my stepmother. No, she is not, but she acts as though she were." There was a subtle change in her expression, a frostiness that passed almost immediately. "My real mother died some years ago."

---

* A rushlight is a candle made from rushes and sold for a farthing, an insignificant sum, and proverbially shedding only a weak, flickering light.

---

† A traditional Irish cudgel.

He was silent for a moment in sympathy. "Who was your teacher before Elsa?"

"Rudolf Salz. You know, the man who was killed yesterday." Recollection brought with it a shudder of revulsion. "I was there when it happened. It was a terrible shock! I was backstage and I saw his face."

"Then you must have known Salz rather well."

"Too well."

Dave caught the bitter distaste in her voice. "I understand very few people could get along with him."

"That's right." Her lips were compressed. "He was the most ill-humored person I ever knew, a vitriolic, sarcastic tyrant. I think he had a sadistic streak in him—it gave him pleasure to hurt people."

"They tell me he was a great musician."

"He was. His knowledge of Wagner was encyclopedic. And he knew a great deal about the human voice and how to use it. I learned a lot from him before it got too much for me. And it was the same with his other students. They all left him."

"Except Hilda Semple and Karl Ecker." He added casually, "You're related to Ecker, aren't you?"

"He was married to Dad's sister, my Aunt Ivy." Pain shadowed her eyes. "I suppose you know what happened—she was killed by a burglar last year."

He nodded in sober silence.

"We were sick for months after it happened. Poor Karl! That was the only time I ever felt close to him. A companionship of misery. He went all to pieces. It must have been a dreadful shock—coming home and finding her like that."

Dave turned his glass slowly on the table. "What kind of woman was your aunt?"

She looked at him quickly, frowning. "Why do you ask?"

"Well, the police never did anything, and—frankly, I'm

interested. And besides, I'm working on an angle that may be connected."

"In what way?" She was watching him sharply.

"It's all very nebulous—nothing I can pin down for you. But my question is prompted by more than idle curiosity, believe me."

She looked away from him, and when she spoke her voice was flat and lifeless.

"Ivy was very sensitive, overemotional, a little neurotic perhaps. She wanted desperately to be a singer, but of course she had no talent. It was a tragic frustration and there were times, I think, when she suspected it, and then she would become despondent, suffering long fits of depression and melancholy. The only nice thing that ever happened to her was Karl. He was unknown when they met, but she worshiped him and had faith in him. His success was a sort of fulfillment for her."

"She probably needed a psychiatrist more than a husband."

"I—" Jane smiled wanly and said, "Let's change the subject, shall we?"

"Right." He made his voice deliberately cheerful. "We came here to discuss your concert. Who's handling the business details?"

"Elsa's manager, Howard Stark."

Dave made a face. "Oh…"

She caught his tone. "What's the matter? Don't you like Howard?"

"Not particularly."

She looked surprised. "But I think he's nice."

"Well," Dave smiled, "don't worry about it. He's not crazy about me, either."

"But why, Dave?"

He shrugged negligently. "For one thing, we don't agree on publicity methods. Or maybe it's just our personalities. We seem to rub each other the wrong way."

Puzzlement wrinkled her brow. "That's hard to understand. Most people like Howard. And he's been perfectly wonderful about getting me set at Town Hall. He knows all the angles."

"But he can't sell tickets," Dave said smugly. "That's my department." He produced a pencil and paper. "Now, let's get down to facts. I want some data on your past history—anything that might catch the public fancy."

"I was expelled from Miss Derwent's Seminary for Young Ladies."

"Ah!" His pencil was poised with anticipation. "What for?"

"Smoking cigars."

He sighed in disappointment. "Seriously, Jane. You haven't been living in a vacuum—there must be an angle somewhere."

She shook her head. "Afraid not. I've lived a very sheltered life. No entanglements. No Italian counts. No scandals."

"Then we'll have to make our own publicity. And since we don't have any time to lose, I think we'd better start tonight. At dinner."

CHAPTER SEVEN

It was a large apartment-hotel that had been constructed around the turn of the century. Rococo stonework decorated its façade. Age, however, had not dulled the building's luster or its air of genteel dignity. Tenants and location, on the southern fringe of Central Park, combined to maintain its fiction of aristocracy.

In her apartment on the seventh floor, Hilda Semple was restlessly pacing the green broadloom, a taffeta hostess gown trailing behind her. Not a single muscle in her face showed any sign of relaxation. There was a look of intense preoccupation in her eyes. Occasionally, swishing past, she would deliver a kick at the leg of some unoffending chair.

From his roosting place deep in a club chair, Karl Ecker spoke soothingly. "Now, *Liebchen*, take it easy. You're heading for a nervous breakdown."

"Take it easy!" she echoed, throwing her arms out. "It's easy for you to talk—you're not under suspicion."

"Neither are you, Hilda." There was a faint trace of amusement at the corner of his mouth.

"Oh, yes, I am. You should have seen the way that policeman

kept staring at me—as if I was the only one who had any motive to kill Rudolf!"

"Tell me, *Liebchen*, you didn't kill him, did you?"

In spite of her size, there was nothing awkward or ponderous about the way she swung around, planting herself ominously close, a thin edge of anger in her voice.

"That's not very funny, Karl."

His manner remained easy, hands dangling loose between his knees. "It was just a question, Hilda. No need to get your wind up."

"I don't like it." Her mouth twitched. As suddenly as it came, the anger left her. "Oh, Karl, I'm afraid of that Lieutenant!"

"Stop worrying. Wait till he finds out about the argument I had with Rudolf last week. A bloody argument over *Die Meistersinger*."*

She was not mollified. "But you weren't bound to him by a contract that bled you white."

"That's quite true. And all the more reason for you to celebrate. Rudolf's death terminates the contract. You're free."

"But they keep hounding me, Karl." Her voice was driven by anxiety to the point of shrillness. "Questions—questions—did I talk to Rudolf between the first and second acts? Did he have the bottle with him? What can I tell them?"

"The truth, *Liebchen*." His heavy-lidded eyes were turned away. "That you were nothing when you met Salz, that he worked with you, developed you, changed you from a salesgirl to a prima donna at the Met. That he taught you Wagner's operas from *Rienzi* to *Parsifal*⁺ and he was worth every nickel you ever paid him. And that now, with success at hand, you were beginning to balk."

---

* *Die Meistersinger von Nürnberg* (The Mastersingers of Nuremberg) is another of Richard Wagner's long, long operas, usually over four and a half hours, first performed in 1868.

+ *Rienzi, der Letzte der Tribunen* (Rienzi, the Last of the Tribunes) was only the second of Wagner's operas to be performed, in 1842; *Parsifal* was the last to be performed in his lifetime, in 1882.

A slow flush crawled up and left her cheekbones stained. Her eyes blazed and for a moment she was incapable of speech. Then she was trembling, and her voice came out muffled. "Oh, Karl—Karl—how can you say such things to me."

He was unmoved. "Because they're true. I heard the fight, *Liebchen*, remember?"

She swallowed painfully. "It was an argument, not a fight, and I still think the contract was unfair. All I wanted was an adjustment. He should have been reasonable."

"Reasonable?" Ecker laughed shortly. "You expected Rudolf to be reasonable?"

She nodded unhappily. "I know. It was only talk. And right to the end I kept my part of the bargain."

"Then you have nothing to worry about."

"But what if they openly accuse me?" she asked in a sudden burst of desperation. "Even if I'm cleared. You know how Van Cleff feels about scandal and unsavory publicity."

His face changed, became blank and unfathomable. "You're quite right, Hilda," he said with acid precision. "Van Cleff has an obsession. The police must be sidetracked. No matter what the cost, you've got to keep them from bringing their suspicions into the open."

"How, Karl?" Her voice was pitched almost to hysteria. "How?"

"By making them believe you were on perfectly friendly terms with Salz."

"It's too late," she wailed. "I've already declared myself. They know what I thought of Rudolf. If only—"

The sound of the bell jerked her around, head cocked to one side, motionless. It rang again. Her eyes looked blindly back to Ecker.

"For heaven's sake!" he said harshly. "Pull yourself together, Hilda, and see who it is."

She took a long, trembling breath and went to the door. When she opened it, Lieutenant Quentin was standing there with a careful smile of politeness on his face. He removed his hat.

"Sorry to disturb you, Miss Semple. A couple of new questions came up that need answering."

"Come in," she said, coldly. "Please do."

Karl Ecker was on his feet instantly with a smile of greeting and his hand extended. Lieutenant Quentin's investigation of his wife's death a year ago had introduced them, and now Salz's murder had brought them together again.

"How do you do, Lieutenant." His manner was cordial. "Just got here a couple of minutes ago myself. Miss Semple and I were discussing a radio program we may do together. However, it can wait if I'm in the way…"

"Not at all. Stick around." It was more than an invitation. "Maybe you can help."

Ecker smiled blandly and sank back into the chair. "Always glad to co-operate."

"You, too, Miss Semple, would you sit down, please?"

There was an advantage to be gained by standing over them. It added stature to his authority, as Quentin knew from long experience. He allowed the silence to become a bit uncomfortable, as if three strangers had been left alone by an inconsiderate hostess. Hilda, patently nervous, reached for a cigarette. Her hand, holding the match, was a trifle unsteady. Ecker sat with a look of polite attention on his solemn countenance.

At last, clearing his throat, Lieutenant Quentin said, "We've come across a new development, one that involves a large sum of money—about fifty thousand dollars in cash in Salz's safe-deposit box.* Plus a rather substantial sum in his bank account.

---

* About $1 million in 2021's inflated values (Williamson, "Purchasing Power," Measuring Worth, 2021).

It was my understanding that he came to this country a few years ago without a dime. Stone broke. He couldn't have made that much money giving lessons. You, Miss Semple, were his principal source of income. Did he receive that kind of money from you?"

She returned his stare blankly. "You flatter me, Lieutenant. Of course not."

"When did your contract with him start paying off?"

"Only last year."

"And your income?"

Her laugh was thin. "Nothing like that, I can assure you."

"This is your first season at the Met?"

"My second."

"And your fee?"

"Five hundred dollars a performance. My contract calls for ten performances this season."

Quentin made a rapid calculation. "Giving Salz twenty-five hundred for his cut." His brows met in a straight line and he peered out from under sharply. "How about radio, recordings, other supplementary sources?"

A half smile barely touched her lips. "A singer's reputation grows slowly, Lieutenant. They were just beginning to pay off."

Quentin's lips pursed. "Then our friend Salz must have had other sources of income. Any ideas on that, Miss Semple?"

"I'm afraid not."

"You, Mr. Ecker?"

The tenor spread his hands in a gesture of bewilderment. "I'm astonished, Lieutenant. I had no idea Salz had that kind of money. He was always pleading poverty." Ecker shook his head. "Amazing!"

"He was your teacher. What did you pay him for lessons?"

"Ten dollars an hour." Ecker smiled disparagingly. "He was not a teacher, exactly. More of a coach."

"You got along with him all right?"

"Within reason. I respected his knowledge. The things he taught me cannot be measured in terms of money."

"But ordinarily he was a hard taskmaster?"

"For most people, yes. A woman like Miss Vaughn, for example, could never get along with him. She was too independent. Salz demanded implicit obedience."

"How did Miss Vaughn get along with other members of the company?" Quentin had quickly seized the opportunity to do a little fishing.

Ecker hesitated. He moved his shoulders expressively.

"How can I explain this, Lieutenant? It applies not only to Miss Vaughn, but to all of us. An opera house is a strange place—a melting pot of nationalities and temperaments. Salz was an Austrian. I myself am half Czech, half English. We have a Swedish contralto, a Hungarian bass, a Rumanian conductor, an Italian wardrobe mistress. Backstage is like the Tower of Babel. Music is the common denominator that keeps us working together in some degree of harmony.

"But always there are undercurrents of antagonism, intense jealousies seething below the surface. Singers are by nature an egotistical lot, convinced of their own superiority, constantly suspicious of their colleagues. Each is certain that he belongs on top and is inclined to resent anyone who stands in his way." A wry smile twisted his lips. "Such a state of affairs, as you can see, is not conducive to harmony or an atmosphere of friendliness. It's like working in a tinderbox. Anything can touch off the explosion."

Quentin said softly, "Aren't you on top, Mr. Ecker?"

"Well—almost."

"Do some members of the company resent you?"

"Possibly. You see, Lieutenant, I'm in a slightly different position. Not all tenors are able to sing Wagner. It requires special equipment. Still, there must be those, I imagine, who would not mourn if I suddenly lost my voice."

"Would you say then that Miss Vaughn is in a vulnerable position?"

"She far more than I, if only by virtue of her sex. Women are more emotional, less stable, about such things than men. Sometimes it obscures their reason."

Hilda Semple came to life. "That's not true." Petulance broke through her anxiety. "People are people and you can't generalize about them. Women are no different emotionally than men."

Ecker moved his shoulder in overweening condescension, smiling at Quentin, who was watching Hilda.

"Miss Vaughn is on top. Do you feel no resentment about that, Miss Semple?"

She said curtly, "Why do you ask?"

He replied in a mild voice. "I'm a detective. When I work on a case I like to understand the psychology of the people involved."

"Am I involved, Lieutenant?"

"You know the answer to that better than I do."

A note of complaint flattened her voice. "I think you're hounding me."

"The word is your own," he said reasonably. "I'm questioning everyone connected even remotely with Salz. You were close to him. After all, the man was killed."

"I know. I was there."

"Is that your only comment?"

"It was a terrible thing for the Met."

"It was a worse thing for Salz. The Met will survive."

"Art always survives," Ecker said.

Hilda took a deep breath and assumed an air of martyred patience. "Just exactly what is it you want from me, Lieutenant?"

"Some information about Elsa Vaughn."

"Such as?"

"It's common knowledge that she was on bad terms with Salz. Did he ever mention it to you?" Quentin's tone was guileless. If she wanted to believe that he was investigating the possibility of Miss Vaughn's guilt, that was okay too.

"Frequently. He was always holding her up as an example of American stupidity. Apparently she believed her judgment was superior to his."

"You know her well?"

"Not socially. We've sung together in a number of operas, but that's as far as it went."

"I'm a little out of my depth here, Miss Semple. Could you tell me, as a point of curiosity, whether Miss Vaughn's voice justifies its reputation?"

He was more interested in the tone of her answer than in its critical value.

"She's all right," Hilda said carelessly. "Good placement and quality, I suppose, but to me her voice lacks warmth. And I don't think it's flexible enough. I've always had the feeling that she was limited."

"The public likes her."

"The public!" It was tossed off with bitterness. "Do you think the public is competent to judge? A public that devours five million comic books a year and never stops listening to jazz!"

"Well, how about the critics?"

She dismissed them with a scornful gesture. "Most of the critics are prejudiced and incompetent."

Quentin frowned, seemingly confused. "According to Frederick Koch, she's one of the outstanding talents of the day."

"Koch is mistaken. And who is *he* to judge? A musical cobbler who waves a baton!"

Karl Ecker chuckled softly, amused by the exchange. Quentin

rubbed the back of his neck. Hilda's opinions, he knew, were the result of an occupational disease suffered almost universally by musicians in all categories, singers and instrumentalists alike. They were blind and deaf to the merits of their contemporaries. He had learned in the last twenty-four hours to discount their opinions.

Hilda Semple opened up in a sudden rush of words. "I'd like to make one thing clear, Lieutenant. I resented my contract with Rudolf Salz—I've already told you that. But I know what he did for me. Everything I am today, whatever my success, I owe to him. I came to him practically penniless. He had faith in my future and he offered to buy a share of that future when no one else was interested. He trained my voice, taught me scores and librettos, groomed me for an audition at the Met, and finally persuaded Van Cleff to hear me. All this on a contingent basis. You would be wrong to suppose that I was not grateful, that I lacked a sense of obligation. I realized and I appreciated his contribution, and no mercenary motives would have induced me to kill the man. I had grown to dislike him, yes. But I did not kill him."

Her last words came out with slow, flat emphasis.

Ecker said quietly, "But no one is accusing you, Hilda."

She turned on him. "Not in so many words. But I know that I am under suspicion."

"We all are." He appealed to Quentin. "Isn't that true, Lieutenant?"

Quentin smiled without humor. "Quite. Nobody has been scratched. The field is wide open." He set his snap-brim hat squarely on his head. "Thanks for the co-operation. Don't get up. I can get to the door by myself. Be seeing you."

For a long moment after he was gone, the two of them sat in silence, staring at each other.

———

Mr. Leonard Opdyke, chief of claims for American Indemnity, was a small man with shrewd eyes in a rather doleful face. His sadness was the result of experience. Mr. Opdyke had lost faith in the integrity of America's policy holders. The swivel chair creaked as he leaned back and surveyed the young man across his desk.

"So you want to know about the Ivy Ecker robbery?" he asked. "And just what is your interest, Mr. Lang?"

"I'm not at liberty to say." Dave Lang leaned forward. "However, I'm working on an angle that may lead somewhere. If you feel—"

"Oh, I don't mind talking about it," Opdyke put in quickly. "We'll accept help from any source at this stage of the game, and no questions asked. The truth is, we're stymied. We had no luck on it at all. None of the Ecker loot ever turned up. Not one single piece. We put out feelers but never got a nibble. We contacted every known fence and shady dealer across the country. Nothing. Of course, the stones may have been smuggled over the border, or even taken out of their settings, which I doubt, since a large part of their value rested in the fact that they were antiques."

He shook his head mournfully. "I knew from the start that this was going to be a hard nut to crack. It always is when murder accompanies the theft. No fence will touch the deal and the crook is forced to lay low. The pro manages to stay away from murder. When an amateur is forced to bump his victim he sometimes gets panicky and unloads his loot in the bay. Then it never turns up." He glanced hopefully at Dave. "You have any connections around town?"

"A few."

Opdyke opened his hands. "I'm free to say this: if you get a line on the stuff we'd be happy to pay a commission. It would amount to a considerable sum in this case."

"Will you answer a few questions?"

"Go ahead, ask them."

"I understand the jewels were all old family heirlooms. How come Stanley DeBrett never put in a claim?"

"He couldn't. They belonged to his sister. Since she left no will, everything reverted to the estate. As her husband, Karl Ecker became the sole heir."

"So you paid off to him."

"That's right."

"And no evidence ever turned up indicating that he might be guilty?"

Opdyke permitted himself a pusillanimous smile. "I wish it had. We're a suspicious lot, we insurance people, especially indemnity carriers... I guess we look like fair game, more so than life insurance companies. Killing someone to collect on that kind of policy carries obvious risks. But dropping a moth-eaten fur coat down the incinerator or leaving it on a chair in the Automat is a lot easier. We were clipped hard by the loss of Ivy Ecker's jewels. And we really worked on that case. But we came up against a blank wall at every turn."

"Then Ecker is clear?"

"Unless he shot his wife with a thirty-two-caliber automatic from a distance of ninety miles."

"And you're convinced it was the job of an amateur?"

"Absolutely. It was badly bungled. The killer let his victim get too close and there was a struggle. An old hand would have avoided that."

Dave nodded thoughtfully. "It could have been someone she knew. She would have opened the door for a voice she recognized. How about her relatives?"

"All right, how about them? Would you like me to hound Stanley DeBrett or his daughter? Do you know how long I'd last?"

Dave shifted his center of gravity and scratched the back of his head. "Have you got a list of the stuff that was stolen?"

"Indeed I have. It was mimeographed and sent out to dealers and pawnbrokers all over the country."

"May I have a copy?"

Opdyke opened a drawer and pulled out a long sheet and proffered it to Dave, who thanked him and stood up.

"I'm merely boring along the edges, looking for a hole."

"If you find one," Opdyke said sourly, "let me know and I'll crawl in with you."

"That's a rather gloomy attitude."

"You'd be gloomy, too, if you couldn't explain to your boss how a fortune in stones simply evaporated into thin air."

"There must be an explanation somewhere."

"There probably is. But the big wheels in this company aren't interested in explanations. They paid off and they want results." He reached out to shake Dave's hand. "Here's hoping you dig up a lead for us."

CHAPTER EIGHT

In his office, thirty floors above Broad Street, Stanley DeBrett stood at the triple bank of windows. He was a tall lean man, prematurely gray, with steadfast eyes and a tight precise mouth. His dark suit was impeccably tailored and sober in appearance. As an investment broker who controlled the financial destinies of innumerable clients, he wore his responsibilities with an easy air of assurance. Late afternoon shadows lengthened across the city as he gazed in preoccupation at the panorama below. Weather-scarred freighters were lumbering heavily in the murky swell of New York Harbor, their cargo booms silhouetted against the Brooklyn shore. Down in the street, oddly foreshortened, people were scurrying antlike for the subway kiosks.

The telephone erupted into sound. He moved to his desk and picked it up. His secretary spoke a name and he said with weary patience, "All right, put her on." The line clicked. "Good afternoon, Mrs. Wells. What's on your mind?"

The instrument buzzed in his ear like an angry wasp. His face tightened into a set expression. He broke into the harangue abruptly, his voice crisp.

"Now, listen to me. You're a widow, Mrs. Wells, and you cannot afford to speculate. You've got a good, solid portfolio. I built it up after careful consideration. The income is small but assured. I can promise you one thing: if you insist on volatile issues, you'll be applying to the Department of Welfare for a handout."

The receiver rattled. He listened for a moment and again interrupted.

"Look here. I know all about inflation. I don't care what you read in the papers. If those financial prognosticators knew everything, they'd be too busy clipping coupons—they wouldn't have time enough to write a column giving advice to other people. I don't want to sound arbitrary about this thing, but you'll have to take my advice or I won't be able to handle your account."

The starch went out of her protest at this ultimatum. After a half-hearted apology she rang off. DeBrett reached for a cigar, trimmed the end, and clamped it between his teeth. A silver lighter stopped in mid-air as the door opened. A transformation came over his face, eyes and mouth warming in a smile. He rose at once, stepping away from the desk to open his arms, as a youthful figure ran forward.

"Jane."

She nuzzled against him. "Hello, Dad."

"Well, what brings you down here at this hour?"

She pulled away to look at his face. "Oh," she said lightly, "just shopping around for some Federal Reserve notes."

He chuckled. "I can use a couple myself. Let me know if you find any bargains."

"Any particular size?"

"The larger the better. Maybe J. P. Morgan has a sale. They always carry a good stock."

Jane laughed and straightened a necktie that was already flawless. "I happened to be in the neighborhood," she said, "and I thought if you were going home I'd ride along. After all, I don't get to see my favorite parent very much these days."

"A pleasure. Sit behind that desk for a moment and make like an executive. Be with you directly." He gathered a sheaf of papers off the desk and disappeared into the front office.

Ten minutes later, in a crowded elevator, they were plummeting to street level. Stanley DeBrett glanced at his wrist watch. Almost on signal a limousine, with a smartly uniformed chauffeur at the wheel, pulled up to the curb. They climbed in and settled back.

Traffic at this hour was clogged and congested, an insomniac monster of steel, animated by internal combustion and remotely operated by traffic signals. Jane touched a button and the window rolled up, insulating them from the din. For several blocks she sat in introspective silence. DeBrett, sensing a mood, turned to study her with critical appraisal.

"Something on your mind?"

She kept her eyes straight ahead, searching for the right words. "Yes, Dad. They—they're digging into Aunt Ivy's death again."

His face suffered a slow loss of expression. The skin around his mouth was suddenly stretched taut. His eyes came up to check the glass behind the chauffeur and found it rolled up. He spoke in a quietly controlled voice.

"What is this all about, Jane? Who is digging into Ivy's death?"

"A young man I met today."

"A policeman?"

"No. He works for Elsa Vaughn."

Stanley DeBrett was frowning. "Any reason for the investigation? Any special ax to grind?"

Her voice had a curiously flat note when she answered. "I—I don't know."

He looked at her hard. "Are you sure it isn't simple curiosity?"

"No, Dad. He—he was after something."

DeBrett's hands, resting on his knees, opened and closed. His intent gaze had not left her face. "And just why should you be so—disturbed by all this, Jane?"

For a moment she sat wordless, still not looking at him. She bit her lips, then swallowed, and spoke in a voice that was barely audible. "I just didn't want you to be upset, Dad. I know how fond you were of Ivy and opening old wounds again would only…" She gestured vaguely.

The car lurched as a cab ahead stopped short to a raucous symphony of horns. In his mood of preoccupied abstraction, DeBrett did not seem to notice. It seemed as if an invisible barrier had suddenly been erected between him and his daughter, and they sat without conversation, strange and remote.

The car pulled up to the curb and the chauffeur jumped out to open the door.

"Ah, we're home," DeBrett said.

The words came off his tongue without savor. Home was no longer a pleasant prospect for Stanley DeBrett. Whatever feelings he had once held for Edwina had long since died, and the pretense of connubial felicity was a sham maintained for outward appearances only.

They climbed the steps and a maid opened the bronze door. Edwina appeared in the living-room arch as they entered, holding a highball in a tall misted glass, her figure languid in a dinner dress of gold lamé. The soft dark hair made an ebony frame for her slightly tilted enigmatic eyes. Her greeting was warm and silken, unruffled by Jane's perfunctory nod and abrupt withdrawal.

She smiled at her husband. "Well, darling, home on time for a change. Highball?"

A negative grunt was his answer as he turned toward the stairway.

"But you look tired," she called after him, not in the least annoyed by his manner. "A shot of brandy might help."

"No, thanks."

She was insistent. "Would you come in for a moment anyway, Stanley? I'd like to talk to you."

He shrugged and followed her into the living room. A crystal chandelier sprayed illumination over tapestried furniture and oil paintings of three generations of DeBrett ancestors. He planted his feet on the deep rug and watched her curl up against a nest of pillows on the huge sofa. His face had the flat quality of a mask.

"I recognize the symptoms, Edwina. You're after something. What is it?"

She finished her drink and set the glass down carefully. Then she looked up at him, smiling sweetly.

"What's happening to us, darling?"

"Don't you know?" His tone remained curt.

"I only know that we've grown apart, that you've built a wall between us, that I can't seem to break it down."

He laughed once, shortly. "Hearts and flowers, Edwina? From you?" He smiled thinly. "We've been washed up for a long time and you know it."

She looked forlorn. "Couldn't we start over again, Stanley? I'd like very much to try."

"Stop sparring, Edwina, and tell me what you want."

She sighed. "Nothing for myself, really. It's for the Met." His face hardened and she went on quickly. "We're running into another deficit, darling, really serious, and I'm afraid you'll have to help us again."

"Not a chance." His voice was flat and final.

"Really, Stan, it's only money, and you couldn't find a better cause."

He shook his head adamantly, his mouth obdurate and inflexible.

Edwina's smile had become forced. "Honestly, Stan, I don't understand. You're getting more tightfisted all the time. Sitting down there in Wall Street has given you the wrong perspective. Money means too much to you."

He said dryly, "And you dislike the stuff. I suppose you married me for my irrepressible charm and wit."

She let the sarcasm pass. "Where's your civic pride, Stan? Really, you should consider it an honor and a privilege to help maintain such a great cultural institution."

"It's a privilege I'm willing to forfeit. Let someone else have it. I've given all I intend to give."

Her tone sharpened. "But I've already made commitments."

"They are your commitments, not mine."

"Will you force me to go back on my word?"

He shrugged. "Get something straight in your mind once and for all, Edwina. The days of support for the opera from private capital are over, finished.* When the Bureau of Internal Revenue gets through with us, we're lucky to have a roof over our heads. Even if I had the inclination to help further, which I haven't, I couldn't afford it."

She considered for a moment, biting her lip. "May I appeal to you for advice, then? This is a financial problem and you're a financial expert. How can we raise money?"

---

* Opera—enormously expensive to produce—has always been dependent on a mixture of financial supporters, from governmental support (especially in Europe) to corporate sponsors to private donors. Despite high ticket prices, attendance revenues have never been sufficient to cover the production budgets. As early as 1931, the Metropolitan Opera developed a lucrative source of revenues in its public broadcasts. Fortunately for opera lovers, DeBrett's prediction of the evaporation of "private capital" was incorrect: In 2011–2012, for example, the Met's budget was $325 million, with almost $190 million provided by private donors. DeBrett's reference to the "Bureau of Internal Revenue" (today's Internal Revenue Service) is unclear. Between 1944 and 1952, Congress allowed a tax deduction for charitable contributions with a cap of 15 percent of "adjusted gross income." In 1952, that ceiling was raised to 20 percent (as compared to 2019, when the ceiling was 60 percent, or 2020, when there was no ceiling).

"By appealing to the public. You've done it before; do it again."

"But that's only a temporary solution."

"Cut costs."

"We have. But there's a limit beyond which we can't lower our standards. The Metropolitan is the leading opera house in the world and we mean to keep it on top. There must be some other way."

"There is. Get the government to subsidize you."

She snorted. "That's silly, Stan, and you know it—with all the money they're spending on defense!"

"Don't worry about the government. They've got millions invested in surplus potatoes and powdered eggs. What's more important, the cultural standards of the country or a warehouse full of rotting potatoes?"

"The government would never consider it."

"Then take a lesson from big business. Hire a lobbyist."

Her lip curled. "That's fine advice."

"Here's more. Without charge. Change your policy. Have some of those fairy tales translated into English. Maybe you'd make the opera self-supporting. Why should people pay for something they don't understand?"

"The Metropolitan doesn't cater to the masses, Stan."

"That's just the trouble. Maybe it should. Try weaning them away from the movies and the crooners. But you'll never do it with a foreign tongue."

"Music is a universal language."

"Not opera. If you can't follow the story, you can't enjoy the music."

"We sell librettos for people sufficiently interested."

"And who can follow the damn things!"

He had her on the defensive. "Lots of people."

"Music students," he said. "I'm talking about the great

American public that shells out a billion dollars every year for entertainment. That's what they want—entertainment. Give it to them. You've got the facilities."

She shook her head helplessly. "You care nothing about tradition, do you?"

"Sure. But look where your tradition got you—on the verge of bankruptcy."

She came up off the sofa in a fluid movement. "Nothing I say seems to make any impression on you. Really, Stanley, you're growing more difficult all the time."

"The cure is quite simple."

"Is it?"

"Yes. A trip to Reno."*

She looked pained. "But I don't want a divorce, Stanley. Can't you understand? I love you. I want you to be proud of me. After all, I—I'm dedicating my life to your happiness."

"Hah! And just how do you figure that?"

She gestured vaguely. Her eyes were large and innocent. "Well, for one thing, I never told the police about that dreadful fight you had with Ivy just before she was killed."

For a moment Stanley DeBrett did not speak. A frozen look came into his eyes and when he spoke his voice was coated with ice. "How do you know about that?"

"Heavens! You were making enough noise. I didn't mean to eavesdrop but Ivy was screaming. I thought she had lost her mind, threatening to sue you for mismanagement of her funds, saying you did it deliberately because you were against her marriage to Karl, promising to create a scandal and ruin your reputation. Everyone in the house must have heard."

---

* Reno, Nevada, was a popular place for quick divorces, where one could become a resident of Nevada (and thus subject to its no-fault divorce laws) with only six weeks' residence.

"Jane, too, I suppose?"

"Of course. She was in the hallway."

Now he understood Jane's anxiety and distress, her unexpected visit to his office, her vague, reluctant conversation in the car.

Edwina was regarding him with an innocent and beatific smile.

"Naturally, Stan, I've never breathed a word of this to the police, though I'm sure it would have intrigued them."

His stare was bleak, contemptuous, and prolonged. He said with no emotion in his voice, "My sister was a sick woman, Edwina. She was nervous, overwrought, responsible neither for her words nor her actions. It is true, her investments had dwindled, but there was nothing I could do about it. I was bound by the terms of our grandfather's will. Her trust fund was limited to certain investments and no changes could be made. Those companies were too old, too conservative, atrophied by bad management and neglect. They kept sliding downhill and my hands were tied. I tried to reason with Ivy. Naturally I spoke harshly to her. I didn't want her to go to a lawyer and make a fool of herself. Nor did I want her airing the family linens in public. Is that simple enough for you to understand?"

The smile was still in firm possession of her small red mouth.

The lines deepened in Stanley DeBrett's face and he looked tired and old. "Ivy was wrong about Karl. I never had anything against the man. At the time, perhaps, I felt that he had married Ivy for her money. At any rate, he was kind to her and that evened the score." He paused, selecting his words with care. "It is true that I did not want the police to learn about our argument. It was a family matter and might open the way for unpleasant complications." He nodded stiffly. "Now, if you'll excuse me…"

He turned abruptly and marched rigidly from the room. Edwina watched him go; she was still smiling.

CHAPTER NINE

Rudolf Salz lay in state.

The Medical Examiner had released the body and a private mortician had prepared it with skilled hands. In death, the face of the late *Heldentenor* was relaxed, exhibiting no trace of his violent death. Rouge brightened the gaunt cheeks and his fingers were peacefully crossed upon his chest.

Flowers were massed about the chapel, cloying the room with a sick-sweet smell. Someone had placed a wreath at the foot of the casket bearing the words: REST IN PEACE.

It was a sardonic commentary. The chapel was like a railroad terminal on the eve of a holiday weekend. People milled about in great profusion—the morbidly curious plus a galaxy of names from the musical world of two generations. And none, it seemed, had come to mourn. This was an occasion for the revival of old memories, and the animated buzz of conversation rose from clusters assembled here and there.

An elderly dowager with blue-white hair burbled to her neighbor, "I heard him sing *Parsifal* at Bayreuth in '35. He was superb, my dear! Simply superb!"

"What a voice!" said another. "His Tristan made me weep!"

And so they went, while Rudolf Salz rested in his box, quite impervious to the carnival around him. Total strangers had come to stare, their appetites fired by the lurid headlines.

To Elsa Vaughn, the whole pageant was a trifle sickening. Death demanded an atmosphere of dignity, not the turmoil of a cocktail party. Howard Stark had brought her and she stood in a corner of the reposing room, watching the false faces as they swam past the bier.

"You're wearing a long face," he said. "You look like the only true mourner here."

"I'm sad," Elsa said. "What a prodigal waste when a man of talent dies!"

"It's been happening for years. Beethoven died. Wagner died. We'll all die."

She smiled dimly. "Does that make it easier to bear?"

"Come now, Elsa. Salz was no friend of yours."

"You don't understand, Howard. His death is not like the passing of some business tycoon whose industrial empire continues its corporate existence without him. When an artist dies he takes his talents with him. Nothing can be willed to society, or even to his heirs."

Stark shook his head. "That's not altogether true. A composer leaves his music and a singer leaves recordings."

"Yes," admitted Elsa, "but the potential for new efforts and new performances is gone forever."

"And a good thing, too. Older artists pass from the scene and make room for the new."

Elsa turned as someone touched her elbow. "Hello, Karl," she said.

Ecker had donned a somber face. "Didn't expect to see you here, Elsa."

She read his thoughts. "Personal feelings have nothing to do with it. I'm paying my respects to a great artist."

"Yes," he nodded slowly. "Rudolf still had much to tell us about Wagner." He paused briefly and then added, in a businesslike tone, "Are you busy later?"

She looked at him curiously. "Anything special?"

"Koch wants to rehearse the love scene between Tristan and Isolde.* He feels it needs a little polishing. He's coming to my studio this afternoon, and it would be nice if you could come too."

"Of course," she said.

"At four, then."

She nodded. Ecker flashed a smile at Howard, bowed, and moved away. The strains of organ music rose softly in the chapel and people surged forward for the services. Stark hung back.

"Look, Elsa, I've had enough. You've paid your respects. I think we can leave."

She nodded in agreement. There was nothing to keep her here. Funeral orations seldom bore any relation to the truth anyway. The record was all down in the book, and nothing could be said at this stage of the game to alter St. Peter's intentions. They moved with difficulty against the tide. As they approached the door, Elsa spied Jane DeBrett coming to intercept them. She greeted her protégée warmly.

"Thought I'd find you here," Jane said. "Couldn't reach either of you on the telephone." Her eyes were on Howard.

"Something up?" he asked.

"Just wanted to talk to you—about my concert." Recalling her own debut, Elsa smiled indulgently. The business arrangements had been more of a headache than the event itself. She linked her arm with Jane's.

---

* There were several performances of the opera at the Met in 1949 and 1950 starring Helen Traubel as Isolde. However, the singer who performed Tristan varied; for example, on January 2, 1950, Lauritz Melchior played Tristan, while on December 1, 1950, Traubel performed for the first time with Ramón Vinay in the role of Tristan. Rehearsals would have been required every time the cast changed.

"Come along. We're going to take a walk and you can have lunch with us later."

They emerged into a world of bright sunlight and traffic clatter, heading toward Fifth Avenue. The air was crisp and invigorating. Endless throngs moved past them. Stark, exhibiting admirable patience, found himself coming to frequent stops in front of store windows, exiled from the conversation. However, the normal mechanics of living must go on. When his hunger had reached an acute stage, he called a halt to the window-shopping and demanded nourishment.

Ten minutes later they were deployed around a table in a small but elegant café. The headwaiter had greeted Elsa warmly, rolling out the carpet.

Howard surveyed the place with approval. "New place?" he asked.

"Been coming here for months," Elsa said. "I steered you here purposely. I want you all to try a new dish." She opened the menu and pointed. "Sauerbraten à la Vaughn."

"How *lovely*," Jane said.

"Is that 'lovely'?" Howard was amused. "Being immortalized in sauerbraten?"

"Of course it's lovely." Elsa looked smug. "It's the final accolade. It means I've arrived. Haven't you ever heard of Spaghetti Caruso, Chicken Tetrazzini, or Peach Melba?"*

"What next? Pinza's Pickles?"†

Elsa's laugh, hearty and uninhibited, brought stares from the neighboring patrons.

---

* Culinary dishes named after, respectively, opera stars Enrico Caruso (1873–1921), Luisa Tetrazzini (1871–1940), and Nellie Melba (1861–1931).

---

† Ezio Pinza (1892–1957) was a star at the Met for twenty-two seasons, and after his retirement in 1948, he became a Broadway star. His most famous role was opposite Mary Martin in the 1949 smash hit *South Pacific*.

The waiter came for the order and deposited a bottle of sherry on the table, courtesy of the management. Stark poured and then looked at Jane.

"Well, young lady, what's on your mind?"

She was hesitant. "I don't think we ought to annoy Elsa with details and—and besides, it's not good form to talk business at the table."

"Nonsense. Half the big deals in town are consummated in restaurants."

"And I'm very much interested," Elsa said.

"All right." Jane smiled nervously. "You mentioned something about a deposit for Town Hall. I know you'll be needing some money soon, and I'd like to know approximately what the whole thing is going to cost. I've got a little money saved and I want to raise whatever we need as soon as possible."

Stark demanded bluntly, "Why don't you get it from your father?"

"She can't," Elsa said. "Let's not go through all that again. Jane wants to work this out by herself."

He shrugged, found a pencil and a piece of paper. For a moment he was busy writing figures. "Okay," he said at last. "The total cost should be somewhere between fifteen hundred and two thousand dollars..."

"So much!" There was a look of dismay on Jane's face.

"At least. Here's a breakdown. Fee for the Hall, printing of tickets and programs, advertising, hiring an accompanist, rental of a piano—"

"Don't they even have a piano?" Jane's eyes were round.

"They probably have. That's not the point. Each artist usually supplies his own—a Baldwin, Steinway, Knabe, whichever he prefers. The company sends it over tuned and ready for playing."

Her brow was troubled. "Won't any of that be defrayed by the sale of tickets?"

"That's your department. We've been all through it, remember? You'll have to brace all your relatives and every friend you ever had. The general public isn't going to shell out to hear an unknown performer. They've exhibited a remarkable amount of sales resistance in the past, and there's no reason to expect a change now. Only after the critics have bestowed their approval can you get any action at the box office. But first you need a reputation."

"And sometimes even that isn't enough," Elsa said. "An artist must develop his individual personality and learn to sell himself. I think some people attend a Stokowski* concert as much to watch his wonderful hands as to hear the music." Elsa paused. "Supposing I lend you the money."

"No." Jane's refusal was polite but firm. "Thanks, Elsa, but my mind is made up. You've done enough already. I'll manage somehow."

"You'd better," Stark said. "The house is booked and the date set. A deposit is due next week."

Jane's expression changed. Quite unaccountably it brightened. There was an odd smile on her lips. "I just had an idea," she said lightly. "Stop worrying. We're all set. I know where to get the money."

Elsa sighed. "Well, I'm glad that's settled. And here's our waiter."

The sauerbraten à la Vaughn arrived in a silver tureen. Steam swirled upward as the cover came off. The aroma set their mouths to watering. The *maître d'* himself did the honors. They fell upon it with a will, too busy for dialogue. Sauerbraten was Elsa's speciality and she had collaborated on this recipe with the chef.

---

* Leopold Stokowski (1882–1977) was a renowned symphony conductor who disdained the use of a baton, using his hands freely to conduct. He may be seen performing in Disney's 1940 animated classic *Fantasia* with the Philadelphia Orchestra.

Howard finally sat back with a comfortable sigh. "I take it all back, Elsa. You're entitled to immortality."

"Dessert?" she asked.

"Not after that. Just coffee."

"Me, too," Jane said.

"Well—" Elsa glanced at her wrist watch. "I have to leave. Rehearsal with Ecker." Howard started to rise but she waved him back into his chair. "Don't bother. I'll take a cab. You stay with Jane." She stooped to brush a kiss across the girl's cheek and was on her way.

Jane watched her leave with frankly idolatrous eyes. "Lovely, isn't she?"

"Uh-huh. I see we both worship at the same shrine." As if embarrassed at his own words, he immediately coughed brusquely against the back of his hand and changed the subject. "So you expect to raise your own money for the concert."

"Yes."

He shook his head. "I still don't understand why you can't go to your father."

She took a patient breath and said, "Because Dad has a block against this sort of thing. It's rather hard to explain. Remember my mother, Howard? She was a concert pianist when Dad met her. She refused to give up her career when they were married and he was terribly lonely during her frequent trips away from home. And then there was Aunt Ivy, who wanted so desperately to be a singer and had no talent at all. She threw huge sums away on one teacher after another. It wasn't the money Dad minded so much as the fact that people were laughing behind her back. He hated to see her making a fool of herself. And now he has Edwina to contend with, all wrapped up in her work at the Met, practically demanding that Dad support the entire opera sin-glehanded." Jane sighed again. "Do you see why he objects to a musical career for me? Dad would like me to live the normal life of an average girl. You know, get married and have babies, that sort of thing."

Howard regarded her quizzically. "Is that bad, Jane?"

"Not at all. It's good. I just want to be convinced that the other is wrong. For me anyway."

Stark nodded slowly. "I know. None of us can settle for anyone else's idea of security—until it's too late."

Jane looked at him quickly but did not answer. They were both relieved when the check was brought, and they left without further conversation.

CHAPTER TEN

Since Karl Ecker lived only a few blocks from the restaurant on Lexington Avenue, Elsa disdained a cab and proceeded on foot. Walking was one of her hobbies. The miracle of electronics had made her voice and her name familiar to countless radio listeners, but her face, unlike that of the movie star, was quite unknown, and she could travel in public incognito, free from that ubiquitous tribe, the autograph hunter. For this she was thankful.

Not that Elsa disliked fame. It was just that she liked privacy more.

A Filipino houseboy with a wide smile opened the door to Ecker's apartment and admitted her into the foyer. She could hear the familiar tenor voice raised in song and she crossed over to listen at the threshold of the living room, one eyebrow raised in surprised amusement.

Ecker, seated at the piano, accompanying himself, was singing "Vesti la giubba"* into a microphone connected to his recording

---

* The aria ("Put on the costume"), one of the most famous of the tenor repertoire, is sung by the lead in Ruggero Leoncavallo's 1892 opera *Pagliacci*, as Canio discovers his wife's infidelity but pronounces that "the show must go on." Enrico Caruso sold more than one million copies of his recording of the aria before 1910.

machine. Threads of plastic curled around the needle as the platter revolved. Listening to him, it occurred to Elsa that Leoncavallo's music was hardly a vehicle for the Teutonic personality. The highly emotional passages required a Latin temperament.

"Heretic!" she said when he was finished.

He turned, grinning sheepishly.

"Italian opera, Karl? *Pagliacci*, no less—sung by a Wagnerian tenor."

He looked down his nose. "One of my frustrated ambitions. How did you like it?"

"Must I say? After all, I have a record of Caruso singing the same aria."

He feigned injury. "That so? Well, I'd like to hear Caruso sing 'Mein Lieber Schwan'!"[*]

"I'll bet he could have done it." She looked around the room. "Where's Koch?"

"Due any minute. Make yourself comfortable." He flipped the switch on the recording machine and brushed off the filings.[†]

Elsa sat down. The furnishings were a little ornate for her taste. She knew most of it had been selected by Ivy and she wondered why, with so many reminders of the tragedy around him, Karl had never moved. But then it was not easy to find a place as spacious as this.

---

[*] An aria from Wagner's *Lohengrin*. Although it would have been unusual to hear an Italian tenor sing the music of Wagner, Caruso *did* sing the role of Lohengrin—unsuccessfully—in Buenos Aires early in his career. He never sang another Wagnerian opera in public.

[†] Ecker actually "cut a record" here, a technique soon discarded by amateurs for tape machines. This involved a lathe that drove a needle to cut a groove in a blank vinyl disk. Like a tiny snowplow, the needle would create banks of vinyl pushed off to the sides of the groove. Before the record could be played, it needed to be carefully wiped to remove this debris. A similar problem occurred with tape recorders. Recording tapes used metallic oxides to record, and tapes notoriously shed metal filings when played. For high-quality sound recording, it was important to frequently clean the recording heads and tape paths to remove these filings.

"Glass of sherry, Elsa?"

"Not now. I see Rudolf made you buy a recording machine, too."

He nodded. "You know his methods. Coaching a new role will not be easy without him."

"No man is indispensable, Karl. We still have Koch."

Ecker slumped into a chair and crossed his knees. "How did you make out with Lieutenant Quentin? Did he give you a bad time, Elsa?"

"Not particularly. I rather like him."

"So do I, for that matter. But he was asking some pointed questions about you."

"Can you blame him? After all, it was the liquor left in my dressing room that poisoned Rudolf."

"Your dressing room?" Ecker was erect in his chair, mouth open.

"Yes. Howard Stark bought it and left it in my dressing room for some reporters who were coming backstage to interview me. We don't know how Salz got the bottle, but he must have stolen it when no one was around."

Ecker's voice went down to a whisper. "Good Lord, Elsa! Is it—could it be possible that the poison was meant for you?"

"Lieutenant Quentin thinks so."

He stood up and loomed over her, visibly perturbed. He turned his palms up. "Then the death of Rudolf Salz may have been a mistake."

"That's not only possible but probable," Elsa said.

He aimed a finger at her. "But why you, Elsa? What has anyone got against you?"

She gave a helpless shrug. "That's the mystery, Karl. Unless someone wants to get me out of the Met."

"Enough to poison you for it?" His tone was skeptical. "You'd never get me to swallow that."

"There have been other incidents, Karl."

"You mean attempts on your life?"

"Yes."

She gave him a brief recital and Ecker was nonplused.

"But who could possibly engineer such a scheme, Elsa?"

"That's what they're trying to find out."

"Do they suspect anyone?"

"Hilda Semple."

He scoffed at the idea. "Nonsense. Hilda is ambitious, but really, Elsa. She may be capable of a lot of things to advance her career. Murder isn't one of them."

For a moment they were silent.

"Karl?"

"Yes."

"Lieutenant Quentin was asking questions about Ivy."

He raised his eyes, his voice almost plaintive. "Why can't he forget Ivy?"

"I don't know. I suppose because no detective wants an unsolved murder against his record. Tell me, Karl, was she very angry at her brother?"

He nodded. "Unreasonably so. I tried to talk her out of it. But that's water under the bridge now. There's no use opening old wounds. I think we ought to forget about it."

"You never told the police?"

"What good would it do? Make trouble for Stanley? I don't—"

He cut it short as the doorbell rang, and presently the Filipino was ushering Frederick Koch into the room. A tall, attenuated man with a sensitive face and wonderfully articulate hands, he spied Elsa and advanced with obvious pleasure.

"Ah, so you managed to come, too. Fine. We have work to do. A lot of work. We will forget everything but Wagner, yes? He gave us the music. We must do it justice. Am I not right?"

Koch did not wait for an answer; he nodded and descended hawklike on the piano. He got himself settled and his fingers moved over the keys, painting a tone picture of a summer evening in Cornwall. The love duet between Tristan and Isolde emerged eloquently.

Elsa and Karl converged. Their voices rose and blended.

It was a long and difficult afternoon.

Koch, a perfectionist, drove them unmercifully, never letting up until every phrase, every nuance, met his exacting standards. It was late when they finally quit. Darkness softened the room. The Filipino had set a table and they dined leisurely. At nine, Karl drove Elsa home, stopping off briefly for a nightcap.

Elsa was exhausted. After Karl left, she was on the point of retiring when the house phone buzzed. It was Howard Stark, calling from the lobby.

"Can you spare me thirty minutes, Elsa?"

"Of course." It never occurred to her to put him off. She was a little surprised to find how natural it seemed to have him dropping in at any hour.

"I'm lining up your spring tour," Howard said, "and I want to run over the itinerary."

It was an hour before everything was settled. He presented a number of checks for her signature and replaced them in his briefcase. Then he went over to the bar and mixed himself a drink and poured some sherry for Elsa and brought it back, eying her critically.

"You look tired," he said.

"I am."

"Everything all right, Elsa?"

She yawned. "I think so."

"Good. Drink your sherry and get some sleep. I'll call you tomorrow."

She saw him to the door, then came back and put a record on the machine. This was part of a ritual. She seldom retired without listening to some opera for at least fifteen minutes. She sat back and closed her eyes. Mario Chamlee was singing an aria from *Manon* when the doorbell went off again.[*] She considered ignoring it, but curiosity took her to the foyer for a glance through the peephole.

Hilda Semple was standing in the hall, a tentative smile on her face.

"Hilda!" she exclaimed. "What a surprise."

"May I see you for a moment, Elsa?"

"Yes, come in." Elsa led the way and indicated a chair.

Hilda Semple shifted uncomfortably. "You're probably surprised at my visit."

"A little."

"I found myself in the neighborhood and I suddenly remembered there was something I wanted to ask you. A favor."

Elsa covered her surprise and waited politely.

"I was talking to Van Cleff," Hilda explained. "Next season he's adding *The Flying Dutchman*[†] to our repertoire and he says he'll sign me for the role of Senta if I can get into shape by then."

"Congratulations," Elsa said, and meant it. She had sung the role before and did not particularly care for it.

---

[*] Chamlee (1892–1966) was the stage name of the American tenor Archer Cholmondeley, who took over many of Caruso's roles. Chamlee was a regular at the Met, giving his debut performance there in 1920 and his last in 1939. *Manon* is an opera by Jules Massenet, first performed in 1884. Chamlee took the lead tenor role of Le Chevalier des Grieux in the Met's production in 1922–1923.

[†] *Der fliegende Holländer* (The Flying Dutchman) was an opera written by Wagner early in his career and first performed in 1843. Senta is the principal soprano role in the opera.

Hilda continued. "Rudolf Salz once told me that he had presented you with a score of the opera that originally belonged to Gadski.* He said it was marked with her own personal notations about stage business and so forth. I think it would help me immeasurably and I would consider it a great favor if you'd let me borrow it."

"Of course," Elsa said promptly. "I'll get it for you at once."

There was no difficulty in locating the score. Elsa kept all her music carefully arranged and indexed. She handed it over with a smile. "May I offer some advice, Hilda?"

"Please."

"This sort of thing was always a bone of contention between Rudolf and myself. I think you ought to look over the notes and then forget them. For all we know, Gadski may have been following directions inherited from someone else. Singers have been striking the same pose and making the same gestures for years. Times have changed, Hilda. I think the opera should keep pace with the whole modern theater. But it can't if we insist dogmatically on following directions set down fifty or a hundred years ago."

Hilda Semple's face was empty of expression. "Some of these directions may have come from Wagner himself."

"What of it? Wagner was progressive.† If he were alive today he'd probably demand productions that were more dynamic."

Hilda shrugged noncommittally and Elsa knew it was useless.

---

* See note on page 15.

---

† Wagner was undoubtedly an innovator. Unlike most composers of opera, he also wrote the libretto. His concept of opera was expressed in the word *Gesamtkunstwerk*, a holistic view of the experience, bringing together poetry, drama, literature, and music with the appearance of the performance. *Tristan und Isolde* in particular is often seen as the watershed between nineteenth-century and modern music. Hitler's appropriation of his body of work (and Wagner's own anti-Semitism) cast dark clouds over his legacy, but Wagner undeniably revolutionized classical music.

Hilda was a true disciple of Salz. Elsa smiled. "Nightcap before you leave?"

"Thank you."

"Help yourself," Elsa said. "I'll get some ice cubes. Sherry for me."

When she returned, the drinks were ready. They sipped them slowly, while discussing the difficulties involved in staging the *Dutchman*. By some strange alchemy the warm glow of the wine seemed to breathe an air of fellowship, and by the time Hilda Semple left, the two women were apparently on much better terms than before.

An overpowering fatigue claimed Elsa almost at once. Her reflexes were sluggish. Invisible weights pulled at her eyelids. She switched on the phonograph, then stretched out on the sofa and felt herself floating through gauzelike clouds. She was dimly aware of the need to rise and climb into bed. She even tried. But somewhere along the line the communication system had broken down and her muscles failed to respond. The cloud thickened. It closed in and swallowed her in darkness.

The lights continued to burn. The automatic player kept Romeo and Juliet singing. These were physical facts of which Elsa was no longer aware. Nor was she aware of other things happening, strange things, sinister things.

For while she lay there, unconscious, in a numbed stupor, the door to her apartment began very slowly to open. When the arc was wide enough, the safety chain drew taut and held. A pencil came through and released it. The door swung open. A shadowy figure slipped across the threshold and listened.

A moment later the figure was moving silently into the kitchen. Presently a faint hissing sound emerged...

CHAPTER ELEVEN

Lieutenant Sam Quentin had a chip on his shoulder. It had reached there via an editorial in one of the city's tabloids. A murder (the paper said) had been committed in full view of certain Metropolitan personnel, and although two full days had passed, the police were still treading carefully, pussyfooting around. The implication was obvious. Powerful influences were at work, attempting to hush or possibly whitewash the tragedy.

Quentin, usually unruffled, had been stung to anger. Sharply aware of his own integrity, he resented any shadow thrown across it. So the chip was squarely set on his shoulder as he left the elevator and strode briskly along the hall toward Elsa Vaughn's apartment.

The chip was knocked off fast enough.

Among other assets, Quentin possessed an acute olfactory sense. Something was definitely in the air. His nostrils quivered and his pace accelerated. At Elsa's door the odor was unmistakable. His thumb roughly jammed the bell. He could hear its abortive clatter and a sense of impending disaster tightened his stomach like a knot. He made a fist and banged it against the door. There was no response. He grasped the knob and rattled it. The door swung open and the smell of escaping gas struck him like a blow.

He crossed the foyer and saw Elsa stretched out supine and motionless on the sofa. His mouth was bitter with self-condemnation as he raced past her to throw open the windows. Cold air stabbed into the room. He sucked in a deep breath and whirled toward the kitchen. All the gas jets on the range were open, hissing. He shut them off and sprinted back.

Elsa's face was pale and still. Quentin's anger came back. By God, someone was going to roast in the fireless cooker for this! If—

His fingers found a pulse. It was faint, almost imperceptible, but it was there.

Elsa coughed. Quentin began to chafe her wrists. He could see the movement of her bosom now; she was breathing more deeply. Color bloomed lightly in her cheeks and her eyelids flickered open. The eyes behind them, however, were dull, without comprehension. She tried to struggle up, but her muscles responded lethargically.

He ran to the bar, broke open a bottle of brandy, and came back with it. He got the bottle between her teeth and tilted. Some of the liquid ran down her chin, but some ran down her throat.

"Easy now," Quentin said. "Lie still, Miss Vaughn." He offered her more brandy. "Try this."

The effect of another shot of brandy was remarkably therapeutic. Intelligence dawned. She realized that she was horizontal and she reached desperately for a nonexistent blanket to clutch up around her chin in a typically feminine gesture. Her eyes blinked and took in the room.

"What happened?"

"At a quick guess I'd say you were drugged. Lie still for a moment."

He straightened and made a quick tour, covering the place

thoroughly, his mind blueprinting the apartment and its condition. He came back, pulled up a chair, and sat down, facing her.

"How do you feel, Miss Vaughn?"

"Dizzy." She gave him a weak smile. "My head feels thick. Otherwise I'm all right, I think."

"Who was here last night?"

"Several people." She groped in her memory. "Karl Ecker brought me home, and later Howard Stark dropped in. So did Hilda Semple."

"Did you have anything to drink?"

"A little sherry."

"With all of them?"

She nodded sheepishly. "Yes, I believe so."

Quentin looked grim. "There's a sherry bottle in the kitchen. It's empty and it's been rinsed out. My first guess was correct. Somebody, Miss Vaughn, slipped you a mickey."

"No-o...but after all, I had some sherry with both Howard Stark and Karl Ecker, too."

"Neither of those gentlemen is your rival at the opera. They may have other motives, and I intend to check—but Miss Semple has a lot to gain by your elimination from the Met."

Elsa was not convinced. "But to kill someone—!"

"Killing was a last resort. Other methods were tried first. People like Semple are controlled by an overpowering vanity. All she wanted was a chance to prove that she could take your place. It became a fixation, and when the minor accidents didn't work out, more efficient methods were devised. The poison that killed Salz. The opened gas jets last night." He began to walk up and down the room. "Maybe she's innocent. I don't know. Even so, my hands are tied. I can't arrest her. I can't pull her in. We have no evidence, no facts capable of proof."

"It just doesn't seem possible," Elsa said in a dull voice.

"Not to you, perhaps. But I'm in the business, Miss Vaughn. When it comes to motive, I've seen some beauts! You don't like Hilda Semple for the spot? Okay. How about Karl Ecker or Howard Stark?"

She goggled at him. "Howard? Are you serious?"

"That's what brought me here this morning. I wanted to talk to you about him."

"About Howard?" She seemed unable to believe her ears.

"Why not? You had a drink with him, too. A lot of your money passes through his hands. He's your business manager."

"He's also my friend," she said a little stiffly.

"That's fine. But you're a woman, Miss Vaughn, and a woman's judgment is often influenced by emotion and sentiment. I'm a cop. The only things I've learned to respect are facts. And the fact is that Stark controls your finances. How much money passes through his hands every year? A quarter of a million? Does any of it stick to his fingers? Is he likely to be caught? I don't know, but I'd sure like to find out. I'd like a couple of auditors to go through the books."

"You mean check on Howard?" The thought horrified her.

"Yes, ma'am"

"That's ridiculous! Howard wouldn't steal from me."

"How do you know?"

"I just know, that's all." This conviction was stated with all the impenetrable logic of a female. "And besides," she added, "Howard is a wealthy man in his own right."

"*Was*, Miss Vaughn. Past tense. He recently suffered some serious financial reverses." Quentin leaned forward in deadly earnest. "I'd like to know if it made him juggle your accounts."

There was a strained expression on Elsa's face. She sat for a moment in silence, considering it, then looked at the detective unhappily. "But how can I do such a thing to Howard?"

"Can you afford not to?" Quentin's tone was inflexible. "Several attempts have been made on your life, Miss Vaughn. A man was buried yesterday as a result of drinking liquor that was in your dressing room. Last night you were drugged in an attempt to asphyxiate you. Murder and attempted murder should cancel all considerations of sentiment. Individual feelings are no longer important. The man or woman behind this is desperate. Another attempt to kill you is going to be made, and don't for a minute think it won't. It's my job to keep you alive. To do that job I have to put everyone, with no exceptions whatever, under a microscope. Anything less would be a dereliction of duty."

Elsa wavered, feeling ill. "If Howard needed money, why didn't he come to me?"

"Pride, for one thing. And if he couldn't take care of his own money successfully, wouldn't it be a tacit admission that he was incapable of handling yours?"

She shifted uncomfortably, debating with herself, while Quentin watched her. After a moment she looked up.

"Not right now, Lieutenant. I have to think about it."

"And give him a chance to cover up?"

Her face colored. "I'm afraid you don't know Howard very well."

"No, Miss Vaughn, I'm afraid I don't." His voice held a note of irritation. "There was a time when I thought I knew a lot about people. Experience has taught me different. People are a feckless crew and human behavior is too complex, too unaccountable. A man can be honest and hard-working all his life and then some trivial incident will upset the applecart and over the line he steps. We had a case last year, a quiet little man, a bookkeeper, industrious, devoted to his wife, living with her in harmony for twenty years, until one day he got a bug in his head that she was cheating on him. At least that's what he said.

"He spent a couple of weeks distilling arsenic out of flypaper in order to spike her tea with poison. Maybe he did it in honest retribution, or maybe he did it for a five-hundred-dollar insurance policy. Who knows? And who's to say when a man skips the track and begins to consider a criminal act? I can't, and I don't think the psychiatrists can either. The point is, Miss Vaughn, nobody really knows another human being. You may think you do, but you don't, because what goes on inside a man's brain is often a surprise to the man himself."

Elsa had been listening in complete absorption. She took a long shivering breath. After a moment she said, "I'm sorry, Lieutenant. I still want time to think it over."

Quentin knew from the line of her lips that she was sticking to her guns. Neither logic nor fear would tip the balance.

He sighed in resignation. "I hope you're not making a mistake."

"So do I."

"It's your life."

She smiled frugally. "And I cherish it very much, Lieutenant."

His eyes encompassed the room in a swift circular sweep.

"You ought not to be here alone. Where's your maid?"

"In St. Luke's with appendicitis," she explained.

"Who cleans the place?"

"I have a girl coming in every afternoon."

He shook his head ruefully. "If anything happens to you I may wind up back in harness, pounding a beat in Canarsie."*

"It won't," she said, without too much conviction, and then added, "You must have searched Rudolf Salz's place. Didn't you find anything, any clue at all?"

Quentin shook his head. "Nothing. Furniture, dust, clothes, letters that don't mean anything. Normal stuff. Only thing out

---

* An Italian/Jewish middle-class neighborhood in Brooklyn—a long way from the glamor of a Manhattan territory.

of the ordinary was the record collection. Brother, he really did collect them."

Elsa snapped her fingers. "That reminds me, Lieutenant. May I ask a favor?"

He looked at her, not committing himself. "What is it?"

"I made some records when I was coaching with Rudolf Salz. He was supposed to return them. They're probably still at his apartment in that collection you found, and I wouldn't want them to fall into irresponsible hands. Would it be possible for me to send Howard or Dave Lang over to find them?"

He considered for a moment and came to a decision. His hand brought an assortment of keys from his pocket; unerringly he selected one and proffered it.

"All I want in exchange," he said, "is your promise to be on guard, with everyone, understand?"

She nodded soberly. "Yes, Lieutenant."

He went over to the windows and closed them. "Be a fine thing," he said, "if you accommodate the killer and save him a job by catching pneumonia."

Elsa exhumed a sickly smile, and waved to him as he left, checking the latch before he closed the door.

CHAPTER TWELVE

Acting Chief Inspector Nicholas Patrick, Homicide West, was pacing his scarred office like a bear whose cage has been skipped at feeding time. In a savage mood, with his shoulders bunched and his eyes baleful, he was ready to snap at anything within reach. The office crackled with tension. He was an angry bull full of editorial banderillos, looking for someone to gore. Every member of the Squad had tasted the blistering lash of his tongue.

Lieutenant Sam Quentin was no exception. He sat on the edge of a chair and waited for the onslaught to be resumed. The best way to control the fire, Quentin knew, was to hold his peace and let it burn down.

Inspector Patrick glowered and leveled his finger. "What are we?" he demanded with biting scorn. "A bunch of correspondence school dicks? New York's finest or New York's misfits? A man gets chilled off in the Metropolitan Opera House during a performance and what do we do about it? Nothing. Some homicidal nut tries to execute a famous prima donna by gas right in her own apartment and who do we haul in? Nobody." He made an ugly sound. "The newspapers are having a holiday. The District Attorney is breathing down my neck. The Commissioner is howling in my ear. The Mayor is sitting on my back. Everybody wants results."

His face changed. It became long and supplicating. His fingers came together in a gesture of prayer and his voice went down to a muted rumble.

"All I want, Lieutenant, is a clue. One tiny, little clue. Is that too much to ask?" He turned the volume up to a blast. "Is it?"

"No, sir."

"You consider yourself a cop?"

"Yes, sir."

"Then act like a cop. Go out and pinch somebody. Clap the bastard behind bars and knock a confession out of him."

Quentin looked at him mildly. "It's only three days old, Inspector. We're still working on it. All we have so far is a couple of theories."

"The Commissioner isn't interested in theories. He wants a suspect. Get him one."

"A lot of important citizens are involved," Quentin told him quietly. "You can't round them up like a bunch of Bowery bums* and haul them down to Headquarters in a paddy wagon." He paused significantly. "But I'm willing to try it if you give me the green light."

The Inspector was having none of that. He had not reached his present position through a lack of caution. He passed the buck right back to Quentin.

"Now, Sam," he said with a placating gesture, "let's not charge off half-cocked. You're handling this investigation and I don't want to interfere. I have confidence in your discretion, boy. I realize this is no ordinary murder case. But a quick, clean solution would be a feather in our cap. It would restore public confidence."

---

* New York's "Skid Row," now largely gentrified.

"I'm doing my best."

"I know you are, Sam." He spread his hands. "It might help if we narrowed the field. You say this Hilda Semple is our best candidate?"

"On the surface, yes."

"Have we got enough on her to close in?"

"No, sir. Motive, that's all, and maybe a little circumstantial evidence. She was the last person to visit Miss Vaughn last night. Poured her a glass of sherry before she left. So it could have been Semple who sneaked back and turned on the gas."

"Did you grill her?"

"Yes, sir. Both sides. I laid it on the line, without finesse. She denied everything and yelled for her lawyer. She swears she left Miss Vaughn and went straight home to bed."

"How did it sound?"

Quentin shrugged. "The guilty always yell louder than the innocent. But I have no evidence to prove it."

"How about Miss Vaughn's manager, Howard Stark? You say he was there, too."

"Yes, sir."

"Have you quizzed him?"

"Not yet. It's a touchy business. Miss Vaughn wants us to use the soft pedal there."

"*She* wants?" Patrick's temperature was up again. "Since when does an opera singer tell the Homicide Squad how to conduct a murder investigation?"

"So far he's in the clear, Inspector. We have nothing on the man yet."

"Sure, and if we horse around catering to people, we never will have anything on him! Or anybody else, for that matter." He made a disgusted mouth. "Who else was with her last night?"

"Karl Ecker."

Patrick folded his brow. "The husband of that woman killed by a burglar last year?"

"Yes, sir."

"Any connection between the two cases?"

"I don't know."

Patrick looked grim. "I never trusted that bird. He have any reason to shelve Miss Vaughn?"

"Offhand I can't say."

"Maybe the sherry was drugged earlier in the day. Anybody else visit Miss Vaughn?"

"Her protégée, Jane DeBrett."

The Inspector had a remarkable memory. "Isn't she the niece of Ecker's deceased wife?"

"Yes, sir."

"My God, the field widens!" He was putting his hand to his jaw when the telephone rang and he unbent an elbow to answer it, barking his name into the mouthpiece. Quentin heard the brief metallic buzz of a man's voice. He saw a transformation come over Patrick's face, saw his hand tighten on the handset and the quick gleam of excitement in his eyes.

"Shoot him in," he said. "I want to see the guy right now."

He slapped the phone down and he leaned across the desk, looking exultant. "A break!" he crowed. "A break at last."

"In the Salz case?"

"No. The other one—the Ivy Ecker killing. A piece of the loot just turned up in a Sixth Avenue pawnshop. The pawnbroker spotted it and brought it over. He's on his way in now."

Quentin caught the fever. He jumped up and turned to watch the door. It was opened by Sergeant Cullen, who ushered a small, sad-eyed man into the room.

"Mr. Irving Sorkin," Cullen said.

Sorkin bowed. There was a kind of gentle dignity in his manner.

He looked more like a Biblical student than a pawnbroker. He was holding a lump of tissue paper which he placed reverently upon the Inspector's desk.

"A pin," he declared softly. "Diamonds and emeralds. A genuine antique, very rare. Only this morning I was studying the insurance company list and so I recognized it at once."

Patrick got the wrapping off a medium-sized brooch. Green and white fire blinked up at them. He glanced at Quentin. "Recognize it, Sam?"

"I'm willing to take the man's word for it."

Patrick said, "Who left it with you, Mr. Sorkin?"

"A young lady."

"Her name." He was half out of his chair. "What's her name?"

"Jane DeBrett." Sorkin dug a slip of paper out of his pocket. "Here is the form I filled out."

Sam Quentin stood motionless. He stared, unable for a brief instant to collect his wits. It seemed incredible. Ivy Ecker had been murdered and her jewels stolen. Where and how did Jane DeBrett fit into the picture?

"Would you describe the girl?" he asked Sorkin.

Sorkin had an accurate and discerning eye. There was no mistake about Jane's identity.

"When did this happen?" Quentin demanded.

"About an hour ago."

"Let's have the details, please, Mr. Sorkin."

The pawnbroker had little to relate. He lifted his shoulders and dropped them. "I was a little suspicious when this girl came in the store. She was acting peculiar, nervous-like. When she showed me the pin I recognized it. A very distinctive piece. She wanted to know how much I would lend her. I offered a thousand dollars. It's worth five, maybe more. I don't know too much about antiques."

"You gave her the money?"

"Not in cash." Sorkin smiled faintly. "One thousand dollars I do not wish to lose. The girl does not look like a crook, but who can tell? A man came in one day what he resembled a bishop and—"

"Some other time, Mr. Sorkin."

"Yes, sir. Excuse me. I told the girl I do not keep so much cash on hand and she can have a check. She took it and as soon as she left I called the bank and stopped payment. Then I called my wife to watch the store and I came right over."

Quentin extended his hand, and Sorkin accepted the gesture gravely.

"You're a public-spirited citizen, Mr. Sorkin. If there were more people like you, this would be a better city. I'll get you a receipt from the property clerk before you leave."

Five minutes later Inspector Patrick and Lieutenant Quentin were staring at each other across the former's desk. The inkwell bounced as Patrick slapped the desk with a resounding wallop. His face was grim.

"How do you like it, Sam?"

"I don't."

"Neither do I. We've been dealt a beaut this time. Stanley DeBrett's daughter. By God, that's something, isn't it? Burglary and murder all bollixed up with high society and finance. The DeBrett has connections all the way up to the White House. How are we going to handle it? Where are we going to start?"

Quentin tugged at his ear. "Why not just dump it in the District Attorney's lap?" he suggested.

Patrick brightened instantly. "That's it. We turned up the evidence and it's his baby now."

"Chances are he'll jump at it. Look at the publicity tie-in—D.A. not intimidated by money—fights to uphold the law—society girl arrested. He can ride a case like this all the way up to Albany."

The Inspector pursed his lips. "Still, it's our job to question the girl, Sam. I think you'd better pick her up yourself."

Quentin did not relish the assignment, but he nodded with an air of resolution, if not pleasure. He left the Inspector and headed down the corridor. Halfway to the door he spotted Dave Lang hustling along to intercept him.

"Glad I caught you, Lieutenant. Can you spare me a minute?"

"Just about. What's up, Lang?"

"You remember what I told you about Howard Stark—that I didn't think the guy was on the level? Well, Lieutenant, I think I dug up some evidence to substantiate that opinion. He made an investment for Miss Vaughn that was a lemon just to swing a commission for himself. He bought a chunk of a football team that stands at the bottom of its league and hasn't earned a dime in ten years. A look into Miss Vaughn's affairs might show a lot of deals like that."

Quentin nodded. "All right, son. I'll check it some other time. Right now I'm working on something more urgent. The Ivy Ecker case."

Dave said eagerly, "A fresh angle, Lieutenant?"

"Our first break! A piece of the stolen loot just turned up in a Sixth Avenue pawnshop."

"Have you nabbed the guy?"

"It was pawned by a girl. The dead woman's niece, Jane DeBrett."

Dave's mouth worked soundlessly for a moment. "You're joking!" he finally managed to gasp.

"No, sir. A pawnbroker named Sorkin just brought us the pin and described the girl. No doubt about her identity."

Lang was utterly and completely derailed. He gulped audibly. "Somebody must have made a mistake."

"Yeah," Quentin answered dryly. "The girl made a mistake. She should never have pawned the pin."

Dave plucked at his sleeve. "Are you going to arrest her?"

"What do you think?" He liberated his arm and was off.

Dave watched him disappear down the stairs. There was a tight constriction around his chest. He had dined with Jane yesterday evening and there had been no hint, no warning. He had kissed her good night, and it remained a high point in his memory. Quite suddenly she had become a factor in his life. And now the thought of her imminent arrest was indigestible. He felt lost, completely disorganized. He was still standing there when a sudden inspiration galvanized him into action and he went sprinting down the corridor to a telephone booth. He plugged a dime into the slot and frantically twitched at the dial. A maid took the call.

"Miss DeBrett, please."

"Just a moment."

He held on tightly.

"Hello?" It was a voice of entirely different timbre; Dave did not recognize it and he frowned.

"Jane?"

"This is Mrs. DeBrett. Jane left a little while ago. Can I help you?"

"Do you know where she can be reached? It's important."

"I'm afraid not. She was carrying a suitcase and left rather suddenly. I don't think she'll be back tonight."

"Oh," he said. "Thanks." He hung up mechanically, feeling empty and numb.

Everything was out of focus. Had Jane gotten wind of something? Was she running away? His brow creased in a fury of concentration. There was one consolation anyway—if he couldn't reach her then neither could Lieutenant Quentin. He sat up in the booth. What was that name Quentin had mentioned? Sorkin? He turned abruptly and thumbed through the directory.

A few minutes later he was in a cab on his way up Sixth Avenue.

CHAPTER THIRTEEN

The window of Sorkin's pawnshop carried an assortment of articles which bore mute testimony to both the credulity and ingenuity of man. Dave looked the place over and went in. A single overhead globe supplied grudging illumination to a musty and littered interior. His pupils had just accommodated themselves to the change in light when a figure materialized from the rear of the store.

"Can I help you?"

"Mr. Sorkin?" Dave asked.

"That's right."

"I'd like some information about the pin you just left at Headquarters."

The pawnbroker peered up at him sharply. "Are you a policeman?"

"No," Dave said, "but I just spoke to the Lieutenant in charge and he gave me your name. I think I can show you how to make some money."

Caution gave way to suspicion in Sorkin's benevolent face. He sidled behind the cashier's cage and leaned on his elbows, looking at Dave with the weary patience of a man who has listened to a wide variety of schemes. "Go ahead," he said.

Dave smiled. This time he stretched the truth a little, without pulling it completely out of shape. "I'm working in collaboration with the insurance company. They promised me a reward for recovering the stolen jewels. And you, Mr. Sorkin, are the first solid lead that's come along. You can have a cut of my share for any information that helps."

The pawnbroker was interested. "What do you want to know, Mr...."

"Lang, Dave Lang. You're a man of experience, Mr. Sorkin. In this business you have to be a good judge of people. I'd like to know about the girl's behavior. Was she nervous? Was she frightened? Did she act as if she knew she was handling something hot?"

Sorkin's lower lip protruded thoughtfully. "Well, Mr. Lang, I will tell you this—there is no doubt the girl was troubled. Maybe because she was never in a pawnshop before, maybe because—"

He stopped as the street door creaked sharply open. A shaft of light jumped across the wall and disappeared. A tall man in a dark chesterfield with a velvet collar advanced briskly toward them in the gloom. Although Dave had never met Jane's father he recognized Stanley DeBrett from several newspaper shots he'd seen. He flashed a surreptitious signal to Sorkin and melted unobtrusively back into the shadows.

It was clearly obvious that Stanley DeBrett was laboring under a strain. His jaw was stiff and his mouth compressed. He was holding a piece of paper in his hand which he shoved through the cage at Sorkin.

"I'd like to redeem this pin."

Shadows formed under Sorkin's eyes as he painstakingly examined the receipt. When he looked up his face was bland.

"But the pin was pledged by a young lady."

"I know. My daughter."

Sorkin smiled apologetically. "This receipt calls for a valuable item. I don't know; maybe you found it. You understand, I must be very careful."

"Nonsense." Irritation sharpened Stanley DeBrett's voice. "Here." His wallet came out. "You want me to identify myself?" He displayed a number of official-looking cards. "The loan was a thousand dollars. Here's your money." A sheaf of crisp bills followed the cards on the counter and he extended his hand in a peremptory gesture, palm up. "Let me have the pin."

In the shadows, Dave wondered how Sorkin was going to keep stalling. But the pawnbroker was a man of ingenuity.

"I'm sorry," he said gently, pushing back the cards and the money, "but I don't have the pin."

"What?" Stanley DeBrett arched back, scowling. "Where is it? What happened to it?"

"It's in my deposit box at the bank." Sorkin indicated an old cast-iron safe against the wall. "I do not have much protection here. Twice last month hoodlums broke through the skylight and opened that box like a can of sardines. I cannot afford to keep valuable items in the store. If you'd care to come back tomorrow…" His voice faded off hopefully.

Stanley DeBrett did not like it. He did not like it at all. But he saw no way to hurdle the barrier. He chewed his lip in frustrated indecision for a moment, and then returned cards, money, and receipt to his wallet. The wallet went back into his pocket as he contrived an awkward smile and informed Sorkin that he would return early the following morning.

The door closed softly behind his retreating back, no longer as erect as it had been. Nor was his stride as determined and brisk. His footsteps seemed to lag as he moved away from the store.

Dave Lang emerged from the shadows. His eyes were disturbed and preoccupied. Sorkin looked at him and shook his head sadly.

"When a child does wrong, who suffers? The parents." He sighed dolefully. "Tomorrow will be too late. I feel sorry for the man."

Dave offered no comment. He was trying to interpret this new development. Jane must have told her father about the pin and the news had jolted him into immediate action. The pin was evidence and he was trying to keep her out of trouble. It was too late, however. The cards were stacked against him. The orders were already out. He hadn't counted on a pawnbroker with principles.

A heavy feeling of doom settled over Dave.

Elsa Vaughn learned about the incident in a rather blunt manner. She was resting from her ordeal of the night before when the bell rang and she answered the summons by glancing through the peephole. Lieutenant Quentin was waiting in the hall. She opened the door and was about to welcome him when she got a rude surprise. He pushed roughly past her without greeting and without ceremony. The granite expression on his face was unsmiling and uncompromising.

With no explanation whatever he started on a quick search of the apartment, his eyes wasting neither time nor space. He came back to plant himself solidly in front of her.

"All right, Miss Vaughn, where is she?"

"Who?" Elsa was blinking at him in wonderment.

"Jane DeBrett." His voice was curt. "I want that girl. Where is she?"

"Not here, obviously. And I must say, Lieutenant, your conduct is—"

"I apologize," he snapped. "Have you seen her today?"

"No." Elsa looked at him curiously. "What do you want her for?"

"Receiving stolen goods, armed robbery, murder. Take your pick."

Elsa gaped, wondering if the man had taken leave of his senses. She fell back and had to try several times before she got her vocal chords operating. Even then her voice was high-pitched with astonishment and disbelief.

"You—you're joking, Lieutenant!"

"No, that's not my idea of humor. I want to question Miss DeBrett about the murder of her aunt."

Elsa continued to gape.

"No, Miss Vaughn, I haven't blown my top. She may not be guilty, but she certainly knows something about it."

Elsa's complexion took on a pale green patina as he told her about the pin. Sickness lurched through her. "Oh, no," she whispered. "I—I can't believe it."

His voice was cold. "Then try to recall that lecture I gave you this morning on human nature. You never know what a particular individual is capable of doing. We presume a person innocent until proven guilty. But the fact is that Ivy Ecker was killed and her jewelry stolen. A year later one of the pieces is pawned by Jane DeBrett. Immediately, she disappears. Something got her wind up and she bailed out. She packed a bag and left. In my book that's generally a tacit admission of guilt or at least of complicity."

Elsa's mouth hung open. "Jane, gone?"

"Gone, Miss Vaughn. Flown the coop. And nobody seems to know where she is. I thought you might have taken her in."

Elsa shook her head, still incredulous.

"Will you let me know if you hear from her?"

Elsa shook her head. "I—I can't promise that, Lieutenant. What I will do is try to persuade her to see you. I think she will listen to me."

He swung toward the door and paused with his hand on the knob. "A piece of advice, Miss Vaughn. My hands are full. I can't be everywhere at once. Watch yourself." And he was gone.

CHAPTER FOURTEEN

Had Lieutenant Quentin thrown a police cordon around Times Square that night, he might have taken Jane DeBrett without any trouble. For at nine-fifteen she emerged from a movie house into the Mazda glare* of Forty-second Street. A glance at the Paramount clock told her that it was still early. She hesitated for a moment, frowning, and came to a quick decision. She took her weekend case down to the subway, checked it, then hurried back to the street and hailed a cab. She gave the driver an address on East Seventy-third Street and he was off in a raucous symphony of ungreased gears, displaying a callous disregard for pedestrian lives.

Her destination, an old brownstone with a high stoop, stood on a deserted street. It was a gloomy, forbidding structure. The neighborhood was dark and poorly lit. From the sidewalk level, four steps descended to an iron gate. Having studied here with Rudolf Salz, Jane was fairly well acquainted with the layout. Without hesitation she pushed through the iron gate, shuddering slightly at the mournful wail of a foghorn in the East River.

---

* "Mazda" was the trade name of a line of long-lived tungsten bulbs first manufactured by General Electric in 1909, but by the 1950s it had become a generic name for tungsten lighting.

The basement hall, long and narrow, traversing the length of the building, led to a door at the far end. Jane went through this into a back yard surrounded by a high board fence. The sky overhead was a somber canopy.

Jane stooped over. In the darkness her groping fingers found a heavy stone. She wrapped her scarf around it and approached the window. There was not much noise as the missile crashed through the glass. Jane held her breath, waiting tensely. No sills were raised, no curious heads craned out into the night.

The hole was large enough to admit her hand. Careful of jagged shards, she unlocked the catch and raised the window. She inhaled deeply, set her jaw, and climbed over. Interior darkness completely swallowed her.

A match broke into flame, barely penetrating the gloom. It revealed a floor lamp, and she pulled the cord. A large room, ponderously furnished, sprang into view. The centerpiece was an ancient concert grand piano. Low cabinets circled the wall, filled with records.

In a quick, methodical manner Jane began to search. The police had been all through the place, of course, but she had the conviction, unshakable and optimistic, that she would find what she was looking for. She attacked the desk first, pulling out drawers and swiftly sorting through their contents. They yielded nothing of interest. Next she went to a closet containing assorted male garments. A hunt through the pockets also proved abortive. She had turned away and was crossing to a chest of drawers when an unexpected noise stopped her short.

She stood motionless, ears tuned. The noise came again—the sound of a key scratching in the lock.

Jane acted without conscious volition. A swift lunge took her to the floor lamp. She jerked the cord, plunging the room into darkness. She moved backward against the piano, her heart whamming against her ribs.

A yellow wedge of light crept across the floor as the door swung noiselessly open. A shadowy figure loomed over the threshold. The hall light dissolved as the door closed. Footsteps shuffled into the room.

Jane caught her breath. Fear stabbed through her. The concentric beam of a pocket torch flashed against the wall and swung around in a circle. It began to move sideways in her direction. Her fingers made a bowknot of distress at her throat to stifle a gasp and she cowered back, shriveling into herself. But the gasp was faintly audible. The beam of light stopped, quivering against the wall.

There was no sound—no sound at all. Time itself was suspended. An aching lump of fear swelled in Jane's throat. The tension was almost unbearable. The beam dropped to the carpet and began moving again, inexorably closer, searching, probing.

The skin on Jane's scalp seemed to curl. She thought desperately: *If I could only run. If I could only hide.* But where? And even if she knew, there was no strength left in her legs.

The beam of light slid past her shoes, paused, jumped back, pinning them to the floor. It began to climb, limning her against the darkness. Jane's heart stalled and then suffered a violent spasm. Suddenly her face was caught in the torch's glare. She stood transfixed, her eyes enormous, the breath clogged in her lungs.

The light moved toward her, closing the gap between them. The hulking shadow moved behind it. Jane forced her lips apart.

Her voice was a shredded whisper. "Please...please..." But the terror that clutched at her throat constricted it so that she could not finish.

The light came closer, blinding her. The stranger was only three steps away; she could hear a harsh, gritty breathing. Jane shuddered with nausea. And then the light clicked out and the room went black. She felt a pair of hands reaching out for her in the dark. She felt them touching her throat. She stood frozen, unable to articulate. And then her knees began to buckle as the fingers bore down.

Now there was no more pain, no more enveloping terror, nothing but darkness....

CHAPTER FIFTEEN

After a dozen phone calls, half to Howard Stark, half to Dave Lang, none of which were answered, Elsa gave up and leaned back against the sofa, nervously chewing the knuckle of her right thumb. Things were beginning to boil and she was on edge, unable to relax. An attempt to read had ended in failure. Her mind simply refused to concentrate and she was not yet desperate enough to try the radio. She stood up and moved restlessly to the window, gazing out at the emblazoned city. Her fingers, absently exploring a pocket, encountered a small hard object. Withdrawing it, she found in her palm the key to Salz's apartment that Lieutenant Quentin had given her.

Why not? At least it was something to do. She would run over to Salz's apartment and reclaim her records. Any kind of action was better than passive waiting. Without further delib-eration she threw a coat over her shoulders and went down to the street.

Ten minutes later a taxi deposited her in front of the gloomy building. She felt her way down the dim basement stairs and pushed on the creaking iron door. At the end of the long hall she paused and touched the bell, not exactly knowing at the moment why she did so. Its muffled clatter sounded faintly. Then she used the key and opened the door.

Elsa gasped. The place was a sight. A floor lamp was lit and it looked as though it had been hit by a Missouri twister. Pictures had been removed and their backs torn out. Desk drawers had been untidily dumped. Upholstery fabrics had been cut and their stuffing exposed. The room was a shambles.

But what really outraged Elsa was the damage to Salz's record collection, one of his prized possessions. They were scattered around, many of them cracked or broken or ground under someone's heel in an act of senseless vandalism.

The police had been here, of course, but this was not their work. The police were not saboteurs. She went down on her knees, foraging. Anger stabbed through her as she read some of the torn labels—Gluck, Journet, Destinn, Alda, Ruffo, Chamlee*—many of them irreplaceable.

With her lips set, Elsa settled down to search for her own records. She sorted through the unbroken platters and finally salvaged two—the "Liebestod" and Elizabeth's prayer from *Tannhäuser*.† She was tempted to filch a record of Chaliapin

---

* These are: Romanian-American soprano Alma Gluck (1884–1938), who married the violinist Efrem Zimbalist and was mother of actor Efrem Zimbalist Jr. and grandmother of actress Stephanie Zimbalist; Marcel Journet (1868–1933), French bass, who frequently appeared at the Met; Emmy Destinn (1878–1930), a Czech operatic soprano, whose voice was better suited to lighter fare than Wagner; Frances Davis Alda (1879–1952), born Fanny Jane Davis in New Zealand, raised in Australia, a soprano who frequently sang with Caruso at the Met; and baritone Titta Ruffo (1877–1953), born Ruffo Cafiero Titta in Italy and known as the "voice of the lion," said to be the only other singer of his time who was the equal of Caruso in celebrity and fees.

---

† *Tannhäuser* is another fine opera by Wagner, first performed in 1845. Princess Elizabeth is the lead soprano role.

doing the death scene from *Boris*, but managed to resist the impulse.*

Elsa straightened up, took a last look at the carnage, and headed for the door. Her hand, reaching for the knob, halted in mid-air. An odd sound, like the whimper of a small animal, came from the bedroom. Very faint, but with a kind of urgency.

Elsa's pulse quickened. Sudden apprehension stalled her heart. Fear, however, does not always preclude courage. She moved carefully toward the bedroom. Her fingers groped around the wall for the light switch. She snapped it on.

Her shock at the sight of Salz's living room was nothing compared to what she felt now. "For the love of heaven!" she whispered.

Jane, lying on the bed, wrists and ankles quartered to the posts, a handkerchief stuffed into her mouth, lips taped shut, was goggling at Elsa with eyes that were eloquent with relief.

Elsa rushed forward and worked frantically. Free of her bonds, Jane tried to struggle up, but lacked the strength.

"You poor child!" Elsa said. "Lie still, don't say a word. Let me get you a drink."

Jane smiled wanly. The water, when it came, was welcome to her parched lips. She managed to sit up. Elsa regarded her anxiously.

"Are you all right?"

---

* Feodor Chaliapin (1873–1938) was a Russian bass who achieved great international success and championed Russian opera. Boris is undoubtedly a reference to *Boris Godunov*, an opera by Modest Mussorgsky, the Russian composer, and which was first performed in 1874 in St. Petersburg. This was Mussorgsky's only completed opera, but it is regarded as a masterpiece. A version adapted by the Russian composer Nikolay Rimsky-Korsakov in 1896 was regularly performed at the Met until the 1970s, when the original version was presented. Chaliapin first performed (in the title role) at the Met in 1921. There is a recording of Chaliapin in Rimsky-Korsakov's version of *Boris Godunov* at Covent Garden in 1928, and the Library of Congress holds Rimsky-Korsakov's manuscript of the "Coronation Scene" from *Boris Godunov* in the Moldenhauer Archive: https://www.loc.gov/item/molden.3326/.

"I—I think so."

"What happened? How did you get here? Who did this?"

Jane looked at her helplessly.

"Suppose we take the questions one at a time," Elsa said. "Who tied you up like this?"

"I don't know."

Elsa narrowed her eyes and said sternly, "Now listen to me, Jane. I've got to know what happened. Who did this?"

Recollection brought a spasm that shook Jane from top to bottom. Her voice was faint, barely audible. "I—I came here to look for something. I had just started when I heard someone at the door. I put the light out and waited. Whoever it was had a key. He came in and turned on a flashlight." She gulped painfully. "He saw me and he came toward me. Oh, Elsa, I've never been so frightened in my life! I felt his fingers reaching for my throat and I...I guess I fainted.

"When I came to, I saw a light burning in the other room. I didn't know who it was, so I kept quiet. Then you went past the bedroom door and I recognized you. I tried to attract your attention. I was afraid you'd leave without hearing me."

"I almost did." Elsa was searching her face carefully. "You say you came here to look for something. What was it, Jane?"

She dropped her eyes, her face empty of expression. "I'd rather not say."

Elsa let the answer stand for a moment. She said, "Where have you been all afternoon?"

"At a movie."

"Do you always pack a bag to go to a movie?"

"Of course not. I was catching the late train to Darien. We have a place up there, you know."

"Why were you leaving?"

"Dad asked me to go."

Elsa controlled her expression. "Tell me, where did you get that brooch you pawned this afternoon?"

Jane gave a start and blinked at her. "How do you know about that?"

"I'll tell you later. It's important now for you to answer my question."

"Well"—she was hesitant—"Dad gave it to me."

"When?"

"About a year ago."

"And why did you pawn it?"

"Because I needed the money for my concert. I meant to redeem it as soon as I could."

"Did you tell your father?"

"Yes. I felt a little ashamed. After all, it was a gift."

"Was he angry?"

"A little."

"Is that when he asked you to go to Darien?"

Jane nodded, looking puzzled. "You're trying to tell me something, Elsa. What does it all mean?"

It was not easy. Elsa felt a wave of pity. Jane would have to know sooner or later. And the blow would be more shattering if it came from someone else. She said, very quietly, "That pin was part of the loot stolen from your Aunt Ivy when she was killed."

The blood drained out of Jane's cheeks. She sat wordless, her defenses gone. She stared wretchedly at Elsa and then put her face into her hands and let the torrent flow. Elsa waited, suffering with her, until the convulsions stopped. She had put an arm around the girl, comforting her.

Suddenly Jane raised her tear-streaked eyes. "The police think I did it, don't they? I'll run away and they won't ever bother Dad."

"Nonsense!" Elsa's tone was sharp. "Do you think your father is going to sit still and let you take the blame? And if they catch you, which they will, do you think he'll let you stay in jail? Of course not. He'll come forward anyway."

Jane looked small and lost and miserable.

"There must be some logical explanation," Elsa said. She put a hand under Jane's chin. "Listen to me. This is no time for charades. You've got to tell me the truth. I want to know why you came here to Salz's apartment."

"I—it has nothing to do with the pin, Elsa. Believe me. It's something personal."

"Between you and Salz?"

Jane gazed stubbornly down at the floor.

"All right." Elsa stood up, and decided to try a bluff. "I'm washing my hands of the whole affair. Don't come to me for help. I can't help you and I won't even try if you hold anything back. I'm finished. Good-bye, Jane."

It worked. Instantly Jane was on her feet, clutching at Elsa's sleeve. "Please, I need you. If—"

She went pale as the doorbell rang, and again began to shiver. Elsa steadied her. They stood motionless, undecided.

A fist banged imperatively against the panel. The doorknob rattled. Elsa took a breath, signaled Jane to stay put, and went through to the living room.

"Who is it?" Her voice had a slight tremolo.

"Open the door!"

It was a bark of unchallengeable authority and she recognized the voice. Elsa opened the door. Lieutenant Quentin was wearing his stone face again.

"What's the idea?" he demanded. "Calling me and hanging up."

"When?"

"Twenty minutes ago."

She shook her head. "But I didn't, Lieutenant."

He came in, kicked the door shut, and surveyed the

destruction. He looked at her coldly. "What are you doing here?"

"I was looking for my records. You gave me a key to the place, remember?"

A broad gesture embraced the room. "Is this the way you usually search for something—tearing the place apart, wrecking the joint?"

"You're wrong, Lieutenant. The apartment was like this when I arrived."

His brows contracted. A double dent of puzzlement appeared between his eyes. He said, "Somebody phoned and told me if I came over here I'd find something interesting."

"Male or female?"

"Couldn't tell. It was a whisper. The party hung up before I could ask questions."

"Well, it wasn't me," Elsa said firmly.

He gave her a hard look, turned on his heel, strode toward the kitchen, glanced in, then steered for the bedroom. Halfway across the threshold he stopped short; for a moment he didn't move.

Then he said softly, "I'll be damned!"

CHAPTER SIXTEEN

Lieutenant Quentin turned, his glare at Elsa so blistering in intensity that it made her wince. Then he advanced into the bedroom. Jane was still seated on the edge of the bed. He towered over her with his hands on his hips. He was obviously controlling his voice as he said, "Well, Miss DeBrett. And where were you all afternoon?"

"At a movie," she replied calmly.

Her control was amazing. Elsa, who had come in behind Quentin, was surprised. Jane's hands were clasped tightly in her lap, but there was no indication that she would come apart under the Lieutenant's onslaught, as she had under Elsa's sympathy.

"And this evening?" he demanded.

"I came here at nine o'clock."

He directed his next question to Elsa. "Did you let her in, Miss Vaughn?"

"No, she didn't," Jane told him promptly. "I got here first. I broke a window and climbed in."

"You broke a window," he said in an ominous tone, a man driven to exasperation, but containing himself with difficulty. He shoved his face close to hers. "You illegally entered an apartment sealed by the police, the apartment of a murdered man. Would it be too much to ask why, Miss DeBrett?"

"I was looking for something."

"I see." He massaged his chin. "Was it necessary to sack the place?"

"It wasn't Jane," Elsa said. "Somebody else came along after she got here and attacked her."

"Sounds like the Perils of Pauline,"* he said sardonically.

"Oh, for heaven's sake! Look at the neckties and the strips of sheeting she was tied with. Look at her wrists and ankles—they're still inflamed. Here—" Elsa reached for a strip of linen but he stopped her.

"Never mind. Don't touch anything. We may be able to get some prints. Did you see your assailant, Miss DeBrett?"

She shook her head. "The room was too dark."

"Was it a man or a woman?"

"I couldn't tell. I fainted."

He rocked forward on the balls of his feet. "And just what were you looking for?"

She hesitated fractionally. "It has nothing to do with his death."

"Suppose you let me be the judge of that."

She pressed her lips stubbornly and remained silent.

Twin bulges appeared at the corners of Quentin's jaw. He put some weight behind his voice, losing patience.

"You listen to me, young lady. I'm not standing for any more obstruction and nonsense in this case! You're going to open up and talk, about a lot of things, right now. You're going to declare the truth about that brooch you pawned this morning. If you try to hold out on me I'm going to pull you in and slap you behind bars. Maybe I will anyway. And don't think I can't do it! I've got

---

* A popular 1914 film serial, in which the titular heroine is swept from crisis to crisis in each episode.

enough on you right now to make it stick. Okay. Where did you get that pin?"

Jane kept her eyes in mulelike stubbornness on the floor, but Elsa saw them swimming in quick moisture.

"Cut the stalling," growled Quentin, "and talk up."

Elsa said quietly, "Can't you see that she's not well, Lieutenant, that she's been through a terrible ordeal? She ought to be home, under a doctor's care, instead of being bullied and hectored by a policeman. I never thought that you, of all people, would—"

"Save it, Miss Vaughn." His tone was curt. "It's no good. I'm a cop doing a job that has to be done." He leveled a finger at Jane. "All right, Miss DeBrett, get up. I'm taking you in. This is your last chance. You can talk now or spend the night in jail. Tomorrow you can hire a lawyer. Maybe you'll get out on bail. I doubt it in a murder case. You'll be taken before a magistrate and whatever comes out in court will be a matter of public record. That's your choice—give it to me now in private, or let everybody have it tomorrow, including the newspapers."

Jane was a portrait of agonized indecision.

Quentin tightened the pressure. "And don't expect any consideration unless you co-operate. With the evidence at hand we can get a search warrant to go through your house or open any safe-deposit box in the family. I intend to find the rest of those jewels if it's the last thing I do."

Elsa knew from Quentin's tone that he meant business. It would help no one if Jane was arrested. The poor child was in no condition to make her own decision.

She said, "Jane's father gave her the pin."

The dam broke again and the water flowed.

Quentin waited. "Will you verify that, Miss DeBrett?" He seemed totally insensitive to her tears.

She looked up, her face lifeless, and nodded.

"Did you know it was part of your aunt's collection when you pawned it?"

She shook her head; she had a quivering, defenseless look.

"You're doing fine," he said grimly. "Now tell me why you came to Salz's apartment."

Her voice was muffled, but the words came through, brokenly. "I went home to pack after Dad asked me to go to the farm. At first I couldn't find my weekend case and then I remembered that Edwina had borrowed it. I got it from her room and started to clean the pockets. I found a check, a canceled check, payable to Rudolf Salz and signed by my stepmother." Jane faltered and then went on a little bitterly.

"I know Edwina. She would never have loaned Salz the money. So I knew there must be some connection between them. Maybe he knew something about her and was blackmailing her. I had to find out."

"Why?"

"That should be obvious, Lieutenant," Elsa said. "Mr. and Mrs. DeBrett were not getting along together."

Jane swallowed. "Dad's hands were tied. But he was too much of a gentleman to do anything himself. I thought if I could only find something to pry her loose, it would mean so much to him."

"All right," Quentin said. "And while you were here someone jumped you."

"Yes."

"You say you're not sure whether it was male or female, but it could have been a woman."

"Yes."

Elsa's eyes were suddenly bright with conjecture. "Then it might have been Edwina. She's strong enough."

Quentin, who had the same idea, nodded. "If it's true that Salz was actually blackmailing her, she might have come back here to find the evidence herself."

Jane closed her eyes and shivered. "My God, I was here alone with a murderer!"

"Probably not," Quentin said. "The killer could hardly afford to take a chance on being recognized. There was too much at stake. He already had the taste of blood—he'd killed once and he would kill again. But you're here, alive, and that means something. He—if it was a he—tied you to the bed, but he didn't want you kept there all night. That's why he phoned Headquarters and contrived to get me here. This man had a heart. He—"

Quentin stopped short and his eyes narrowed in speculation.

Elsa held her breath. She knew what he was thinking. Stanley DeBrett, too, was involved. Maybe he was the nocturnal invader who, not wanting to hurt his own daughter, had tied her up and then made sure of her liberation.

Elsa said, "May I take Jane home now, Lieutenant?"

He shook his head. "Sorry, Miss Vaughn. I'm afraid she'll have to make a statement to the District Attorney. After all, she's a material witness."

He went into the living room and they listened while he dialed a number.

"Let me talk to Sergeant Cullen," he said. And then, a moment later, "Cullen, take a squad car and pick up Stanley DeBrett. You heard me. Stanley DeBrett. I want him down at Headquarters within the next thirty minutes."

CHAPTER SEVENTEEN

Mr. Mark Simon, the Assistant District Attorney especially assigned to the case, was on the offensive. He was young, eager, and resolute. He was also keenly aware of his official status. The vigorous prosecution of a case like this might lead anywhere. So he had removed his gloves and come out swinging. He only wished there were some newspaper reporters on hand to see him in action. He was going to prove that money and social position meant nothing to him, that special privilege did not exist in New York County, that in him the people had an aggressive and incorruptible public defender.

On the other hand, Inspector Nicholas Patrick, with characteristic prudence, had decided to take a back seat and he had pulled Sam Quentin down alongside him. The D.A.'s office had the ball and he was satisfied to let them carry it. He stayed behind his desk and waited for the kickoff.

Stanley DeBrett stood in the middle of the floor, tired but erect. His manner was one of complete detachment. The one call permitted him had not been made to his attorneys, for the Wall Street firm of Corcoran, Mead, Millikan & Schwartz was totally unequipped to handle any case involving the Code of Criminal

Procedure, their specialty limiting them to that particular type of banditry belonging exclusively to high finance. He faced young Mr. Mark Simon with a patronizing air of tolerance.

"What it boils down to very simply," said the Assistant District Attorney, "is this: either you did or did not give that pin to your daughter. If she lied, if you did not give it to her, then our job is clear. We'll have to hold her on suspicion of homicide."

He was pleased with the way he had phrased it. It put the financier on the spot so gracefully.

"I gave it to her," DeBrett said.

"You admit that."

"I do."

"And you also admit that it was part of your sister's collection?"

"I do."

Mark Simon glanced at the police stenographer to make sure he was getting everything down. He permitted a note of irony to sharpen his voice, as if any forthcoming explanation would be a lie.

"Can you explain how the pin came into your possession?"

"I think so. When I got here I made a telephone call. Would you see if a Mr. Albert Barbizon is outside?"

Quentin rose tiredly and went to the door. In a moment he was back, ushering a small, gnomelike man into the office. Mr. Albert Barbizon was a smiling fashion-plate in Oxford gray and striped trousers, with fawn-colored spats setting off the gleam of dark shoes. He was ill at ease in these surroundings and the smile was forced.

Stanley DeBrett nodded briefly. "Would you tell these gentlemen what your occupation is, Mr. Barbizon?"

"Certainly. I am a dealer in rare gems." He had a slight but unidentifiable accent.

"Am I a customer of yours?"

"A valued one, Mr. DeBrett. You have honored my establishment many times."

"Would you take a look at that pin on the Inspector's desk?" DeBrett waited while Barbizon turned it over in his hands, then asked, "Have you ever seen it before?"

"Oh, yes." The reply was prompt and unequivocal.

"How many times?"

"Twice. Once when it was brought to me by your sister for cleaning and repair, and again just before she—er—passed away." He made a disparaging gesture. "It seems she was financially embarrassed, temporarily short of funds, and wanted to sell the brooch."

"Did you buy it?"

"On the spot. At the price she asked it was a bargain."

"What did you do then?"

"Why, I recognized the pin as part of a family collection and I called you, Mr. DeBrett. I thought you might be interested in buying it back."

"Was I?"

"Indeed. You were eager. We concluded the arrangements right there and I sent the pin over to you on the following day."

As this dialogue proceeded, Mark Simon kept deflating like a tire with a slow leak. Suddenly he pulled himself together. He was not running for cover yet. But the blood was high in his cheeks and he pointed a slightly unsteady finger at Barbizon.

"Did you have any conversations with Mr. DeBrett about this before he called you from Headquarters?"

Barbizon drew himself erect, a bantam rooster with a bristling coxcomb. "If you're trying to insinuate that I'm lying in order to protect him because of some—"

"I'm trying to learn the truth. How did he pay you for the pin—in cash?"

"No, sir. By check."

"Which you deposited?"

"Yes, sir."

Simon spun around and glared defiantly at Stanley DeBrett. "Can you produce the check?"

"Possibly. If I still have last year's vouchers around."

"I want to see it." Chagrin had raised his voice. "I want to see the date it was canceled. And I want to know why, if that brooch came into your possession honestly, you were so anxious to redeem it from the pawnbroker this afternoon!"

DeBrett remained cool. "Any charge against me rests on the premise that I got the pin illegally. Since that premise has collapsed, I don't feel I owe you any further explanation." He paused. "Just to enlighten you, however, the pin was a family heirloom and I thought it wise to get it out of hock at once. Does that satisfy you?"

"No, sir, it does not." There was a note of bluster in the District Attorney's voice. "I'm not at all satisfied. There's more here than meets the eye. Why did you order your daughter to leave the city when you learned what she had done?"

"Order her? I merely suggested. I was afraid something like this might happen. My daughter is a sensitive girl. I didn't want to expose her to your cross-examination." He smiled thinly. "The bureaucratic personality is quite incapable of handling such matters with delicacy. And now, gentlemen, even if you're not satisfied, I'd like to collect my daughter and take her home."

Sam Quentin was willing to admit defeat. He rose wearily and said, "Sorry to have troubled you, Mr. DeBrett. You understand—"

"That's quite all right, Lieutenant."

"Your daughter is waiting downstairs."

"Thank you." He turned and marched stiffly through the door with Albert Barbizon trotting along at his heels.

The three city employees sat and stared at each other with sour expressions.

"Well, that spreads it out in all directions again," Quentin muttered. "We're back in the swamp."

Simon, glowering darkly, said in a bitter tone, "You put me in one hell of a spot, Lieutenant."

"Don't blame him," Patrick snarled. "Your office demanded to be notified of all developments as they arose. Okay, we notified you. You came charging up here before we had a chance to follow it through. Now relax. You got away easy. Suppose we had locked him up and he pulled Barbizon out of his hat as a surprise witness in court. You'd have been laughed off the D.A.'s staff—so throttle down, mister."

Simon's mouth was pinched. "I'm not through yet. No, sir! Not by a long shot. I still think there's something fishy about that family and I'm going to keep right on investigating."

"That's your privilege. How about it, Sam? Do you think they're in the clear?"

Quentin looked thoughtful. "I've still got a couple of questions that need answering."

But he knew they would have to wait until morning. He couldn't go barging in on Edwina DeBrett at this hour, even if she had paid Rudolf Salz five thousand dollars.

CHAPTER EIGHTEEN

Elsa Vaughn was resting. According to her wrist watch, an embarrassingly expensive bauble presented to her by a South American admirer during a tour through the Argentine some years ago, she still had two hours before appearing at the Met for a matinee performance of *Tristan und Isolde*. She had dined lightly. The single lamb chop, while it barely provided the minimum caloric requirements, was a guarantee that she would be able to handle her voice without any gastric disturbances.

She filled her lungs and let her voice run up the scale. She tried a high C. The tone seemed a little burry. A worried frown appeared instantly across her brow. The threat of a cold hovers continually over a professional singer. She hurried to the bathroom and sprayed her throat with antiseptic.

Back in the living room, relaxing, a package caught her eye. It held the two records she had taken from Salz's apartment. She took them out, raised the lid of her phonograph, and placed them on the automatic changer. A third record was already on the turntable. She touched the switch and adjusted the control for medium volume.

Amelita Galli-Curci was singing the "Shadow Song" from

Dinorah.[*] It was a record that had been cut many years ago, but despite the tinny flavor the voice came through, rich and warm. Elsa closed her eyes and leaned back against the sofa to enjoy it.

The phone rang and she stretched her hand. "Hello."

"Elsa?"

She recognized the voice. "Yes, Karl."

"Good news." He was excited. "I just got a cable from Bayreuth. They want me to sing at the Festival this year and they inquired about you. Can you do the *Ring* with me? Are you free to go abroad?"

The idea appealed to Elsa, but she said, "I don't know, Karl. We'll have to ask Howard. I'd love to make the trip if we haven't any previous commitments."

"Couldn't they be canceled?"

"That depends. Howard is driving me to the Met. We can talk to him there. If there's any chance at all I'd—Just a moment, there's the doorbell. That's probably Howard now. Hold on a moment." She put the phone down and went to the door. At that moment, Galli-Curci finished the "Shadow Song" and the record changer dropped a new platter onto the turntable.

A strange phenomenon occurred. Elsa was expecting to hear her own rendition of Elizabeth's prayer from *Tannhäuser.* But the voice coming out of the speaker was not Elsa's voice, nor was the song an aria from *Tannhäuser.* Instead, some soprano was yodeling the Tosti ballad, "Good-bye Forever,"[+] in a voice possessing more

---

* Galli-Curci (1882–1963) was an Italian coloratura soprano whose records were very popular. She recorded "The Shadow Song" in Italian ("Ombra leggiera") twice, in 1917 and again in 1925. *Dinorah* is an 1859 French comic opera by Giacomo Meyerbeer. The 1917 recording is available at the Library of Congress website: https://www.loc.gov /item/jukebox-24080/.

+ The sentimental song "Good Bye!" was written in 1908 by the Italian songwriter Paolo Tosti (1846–1916), based on a poem by George John Whyte-Melville (1821– 1878). It was recorded by Caruso, Melba, and many others.

volume than quality. There was no orchestral background, no piano accompaniment. But there was something vaguely familiar about the voice though Elsa could not at the moment place it.

She opened the door and Howard came in, frowning at the machine with a sour expression. "For God's sake! Who the devil is that?"

"I don't know. Awful, isn't it? One of my labels got pasted on by mistake. Oh...Karl Ecker is on the phone—he wants to talk to you."

Stark crossed over. While he was in conference with the mouthpiece, Elsa listened to the record. The rendition was so tearful and dramatic that she felt embarrassed. Her face was a study in concentrated perplexity.

Howard hung up and said, "Elsa, will you shut that thing off or get me some ear plugs. I'm only human and—" The phone rang again and he got her signal to answer it. He spoke briefly and looked up. "Jane wants to talk to you."

Elsa took it. "Hello, darling. Are you all right?"

"Oh, yes." Jane's voice was lively. "Dad's here and he wants to thank you for taking care of me last night."

"Fine. Put him on."

Stanley DeBrett was obviously under restraint. Not usually given to demonstrations of emotion, he kept his words of appreciation calm and a little detached. In the middle of a sentence he broke it off to inquire without preamble, "Who is that singing?"

"It's a record," Elsa told him. "I can't identify the voice."

Howard had gone over to the machine. He flipped the switch and the voice petered out in a squawk as the motor died. Stanley DeBrett was saying, "We're going to hear *Tristan und Isolde* this afternoon. We'll be seeing you backstage later."

"I'll be looking for you." Elsa said good-bye and hung up. Howard came over and sat down beside her.

"How badly do you want the engagement at Bayreuth, Elsa?"

"Very much."

"You can make it if we cancel the Cleveland and St. Louis recitals."

"Oh, no." She shook her head firmly. "Not Cleveland and St. Louis. Some of my staunchest admirers are there and I wouldn't disappoint them for Bayreuth, Salzburg, and Covent Garden all rolled into one package."

"Perhaps we can set the dates ahead a little and catch a plane across."

"Now, Howard, you know how I feel about planes. You're not getting me to defy the laws of gravity."

He was very patient. "Look, Elsa, when your number's up, it's up."

"Yes, and what if it's the pilot whose number is up? I'd be in a fine pickle."

Stark met this pellet of wisdom with a shrug of resignation. Elsa was willing to ride along on the wheels of progress in all directions except up. He avoided pressure. She would not have heard him anyway, for she put her head back without warning and cut loose with a note that rang in his ears.

"That's nice," he said when she was finished. "A preview for my benefit?"

She smiled. "Just warming up. Singers have to do it before a performance just like baseball players before a game."

CHAPTER NINETEEN

The door to Stanley DeBrett's residence had a knocker in the shape of a boar's head. It was purely ornamental and Quentin ignored it. He punched the bell and waited. A maid opened the door, took his hat, and conducted him on a tour that ended in a modest library where Stanley DeBrett stood waiting, his manner cool but not hostile. He held out his wrists.

"Do you want to handcuff me this time, Lieutenant?"

Quentin did not smile. He merely shook his head. DeBrett raised an eyebrow. "A social call?"

"Still business. This time I want to interview your wife."

"With reference to what?"

"I'd prefer to discuss that with her."

DeBrett stared at him. Quentin's face gave no information. DeBrett turned and reached for a pullcord near the window. It summoned the maid who listened blank-faced to her instructions and then disappeared. The two men waited through a moment of uncomfortable silence.

The door opened and Edwina glided into the room. Poised and outwardly serene, she divided a bright smile between them. "I understand someone wants to talk to me."

Her husband said, with no expression in his voice, "You remember Lieutenant Quentin, Edwina. He'd like to ask you a few questions."

She turned patiently and waited.

Quentin shifted his feet, sizing her up. But there was nothing to see. Her face was innocent and artless. He said, "How well did you know Rudolf Salz, Mrs. DeBrett?"

She shrugged carelessly. "Only by sight as a personality around the Met."

"You knew that he was a voice teacher?"

"Oh, yes."

"And that he had once taught both your sister-in-law and your stepdaughter?"

She looked at him, puzzled. "Yes, of course."

"He was not a friend of yours?"

"Hardly."

"Nor an enemy?"

"Doesn't that necessarily follow," she asked sweetly, "if I barely knew the man?"

His eyes were direct. She had sprung the trap herself.

"Then I hope you'll be able to explain something," he said quietly. "If Salz was neither your friend nor your enemy, why did you pay him five thousand dollars?"

She tried to keep her smile going. It hung crookedly. Then she widened her eyes and asked in amazement, "I paid Rudolf Salz five thousand dollars?"

"By check, Mrs. DeBrett. Drawn on your account, canceled by your bank."

The smile was gone and the line of her mouth straightened out. "It must be a forgery."

Quentin shook his head. "That's a bad hand, Mrs. DeBrett. Throw it in. We can prove otherwise too easily."

She made a bewildered gesture. "But I don't understand. You mean you actually have such a check?"

He extracted it from his pocket and held it in front of her.

She swallowed uncertainly. "It—it looks like my signature. Where did you get it?"

"Through legal channels. And we can use it in evidence if we have to."

She looked at her husband, saw his rigidly controlled face, and veered back to Quentin. Her forehead was wrinkled. "I'm a bit confused. Evidence of what?"

"That's what I intend to find out."

The instant he spoke, Quentin realized he had made a mistake. Now she knew he was in the dark; he should have kept her dangling. Edwina DeBrett exhaled in relief. She tapped her forehead as if to prod her memory.

"Really, Lieutenant, I donate money to so many worthy causes, it's quite impossible to remember them all. Mr. Salz must have come to me in serious need of funds."

"Another bad hand, Mrs. DeBrett. Don't play it. Salz didn't need your money. He had plenty of his own."

Her eyes were shocked. "Then he must have lied. What a dreadful greedy old man!"

Color flushed through Quentin's neck. His patience was wearing thin. He said grimly, "Look here, Mrs. DeBrett, you seem to think that your social position gives you some kind of immunity. You're wrong. Rudolf Salz was murdered. I intend to examine every facet of the man's life, and I can promise you that we're going to find out exactly what that money was paid for."

She moved her shoulders indifferently. "I suppose that's your duty, Lieutenant. I can't remember myself, and I don't think Salz is very likely to tell you."

This was a situation that excluded levity and Quentin was

not amused. "No man lives in a vacuum, Mrs. DeBrett. We'll keep searching."

"I wish you luck."

He was holding himself in. "You sound confident. Is it because you have already searched? Was it you in Salz's apartment last night? Did you tie Jane up and then call the police to set her free? A stranger wouldn't have cared. You might."

She switched suddenly to her husband, eyes round. "This is all news to me. Jane tied up? Where? Did you know about it, Stanley?"

He neither nodded nor shook his head. His face remained a blank, hard mask. She turned back to Quentin.

"What time did all this happen?"

"About nine o'clock."

She looked relieved. "I was right here at home, watching television. Wasn't I, darling?"

"I don't know," DeBrett said curtly. "I got home late."

"Oh, then it must have been the night before." She was not a bit annoyed by the contradiction.

Quentin stared at them, first one, then the other. The door opened and a voice said, "Dad, we'll be late if—" Jane was halfway across the threshold before she spied Quentin. "Oh, I'm sorry. I didn't know you were busy." She started to back out.

"That's all right," DeBrett said. "I'm sorry, Lieutenant. We're due at the opera in fifteen minutes."

CHAPTER TWENTY

The house had been sold out for a week. An eager audience over-flowed through the orchestra, boxes, mezzanine, family circle, and gallery, intently listening to the first act of *Tristan und Isolde* as it unfolded. Among all of Richard Wagner's operas this one perhaps inspires the most fanatical devotion. Woven through the entire score is a theme of almost intolerable longing, climaxed by the most ecstatic love song in all musical literature—the impassioned "Liebestod."

Elsa Vaughn was singing Isolde to Karl Ecker's Tristan, with Hilda Semple as Brangäne,* and their voices were borne aloft on orchestral music of unimaginable beauty. The two principals had just drunk a love potion and were in each other's arms when Brangäne, in despair, finally managed to warn them that the ship bearing them to Cornwall had sighted land. The curtain fell as officers and crew were seen pointing to the shore and shouting their greetings.

A thunder of applause echoed through the house, impetuous and sustained.

---

* Brangäne is the second lead soprano role but is often sung by a mezzo-soprano (played by mezzo-soprano Blanche Thebom in the December 1, 1950, Met production).

Aaron Van Cleff was waiting for Elsa when she came in to the wings and he drew her to one side. "Will you come up to my office for a moment, Elsa? Someone wants to talk to you."

She looked at him in surprise. "During a performance, Aaron? I have to change."

He shrugged helplessly. "It's Lieutenant Quentin. He insisted and promised not to keep you long."

"Why doesn't he come to my dressing room?"

"Because he didn't want to be interrupted."

Elsa nodded in resignation and picked up her trailing gown. She found Lieutenant Quentin standing at the window. He apologized briefly and came to the point at once.

"Sorry to disturb you at this time, Miss Vaughn, but it can't be helped. I want some information and I want it fast. I think you can help me and that you will help me. About Edwina DeBrett. A short profile."

She caught the grim expression on his face. "You don't believe that—"

He cut her off with a sharp gesture. "I don't want to keep you any longer than necessary. Mrs. DeBrett's background, please."

Elsa briefly marshaled her facts. "Here goes," she said. "Edwina was born into wealth. She had a rich and doting father and as a young girl she had everything she wanted. And then came the stock market crash in '29, and all that was changed. Her father died some months later. Her mother was already dead. It left Edwina to exist as best she could on handouts from relatives. I think the experience had its effect; it made her hard and ambitious and selfish. She set a goal for herself and went after it with all the ammunition at her command. The goal was money and social position and she got them when she captured Stanley DeBrett."

"Did she love the man?"

Elsa shook her head emphatically. "Not now or ever."

"Any extracurricular romantic entanglements?"

"None she would advertise, Lieutenant. Their marriage has been on the rocks for years. It would founder completely if he ever got anything on her. So of course she would be discreet, or at least cautious."

He nodded abruptly. "Thank you, Miss Vaughn. I think that covers it."

She searched his face for a moment, then left the office. She reached the backstage corridor, hurrying along to her dressing room. Stagehands were hammering on the set, but she was only distantly aware of the noise. What was on Lieutenant Quentin's mind? What had he learned? Questions were still crowding her mind when she opened the door to her dressing room.

Momentum carried her inside and shock stopped her short.

Someone had usurped her quarters. Someone was in her chair—Hilda Semple, to be exact. She sat with her blonde head slumped forward on the dressing table, a wavering line of crimson glistening at the bullet hole.

The sight paralyzed all of Elsa's muscles except those which control articulation. How many decibels went into her scream, as the pivot of her jaw swung open, no one will ever know. The mechanical instruments that measure sound were not at the moment available. Powered by twenty years spent in developing her lungs, larynx, and diaphragm, fortified by countless Valkyrie war cries, it was an awe-inspiring sound that must have agitated seismographs across half the continent. For the first time in operatic history a dramatic soprano hit an F above high C.

Singers often feel a compulsion to reassure themselves that no mysterious malady has suddenly affected the vocal chords, so the sound of vocal exercises is not uncommon at the Met. Still no one within earshot could mistake Elsa's caterwaul for anything but what it was—a blast of pure horror.

Stagehands, singers, electricians, converged on her dressing room from all directions. They jammed the narrow corridor, milling about, shouting questions. It was Lieutenant Quentin, shouldering his way through, who took command. He took one glance inside the dressing room, then growled an order and drove them back, shutting the door against their goggling faces.

Elsa, still staring hypnotically, had her mouth open for another scream. Quentin's palm left a red streak across her cheek. His fingers gripped her shoulders, steadying her.

"Hang on, Miss Vaughn. Take it easy."

It broke the spell. The hysteria that had been mounting in her eyes began to recede. She turned to him, her face dull with shock. "Is she...can't you do something?"

"Not now. No one can. We'll be swamped in a minute—tell me what happened."

Elsa shuddered. Her throat worked. She shook her head and said, "After I left you I came straight here. She was like this when I opened the door."

"Nothing was touched?"

"Not by me," she said in a whisper.

He gazed rapidly around the room and nodded. "Well, it looks like I've saved your life again."

Her eyes were torpid, uncomprehending. "What do you mean?"

"It's quite simple. Hilda Semple was sitting at your dressing table, where you should have been. The angle of vision from that door does not permit a view through the mirror. Anyone opening it a crack would naturally mistake her for you. From the back there is a close resemblance. Hilda Semple has your figure and the same color hair. You were supposed to have been the target—only you were upstairs in Van Cleff's office with me."

Comprehension came back into Elsa's eyes. She began to breathe deeply.

Quentin went on. "Someone is growing desperate. Time is running out. He wants you dead and he can't afford to wait, and that's why he took a chance. What happened is clear enough: the killer was loitering in the corridor. When the road was clear he opened the door, aimed quickly, and fired."

Her throat was parched. "But no one heard a shot."

"The gun must have had a silencer."

She grasped his sleeve urgently. "There must be fingerprints on the doorknob!"

He shook his head. "Not after all those people wrestled with it."

Elsa shook her head. "But what was Hilda doing in my dressing room?"

"We can only guess. Probably she had something she wanted to tell you."

Someone rapped a set of frantic knuckles against the door panel. Exasperation crossed Quentin's face. He pulled the door open, blocking the view. Van Cleff, mopping his streaming brow, appealed to him.

"Is it true, Lieutenant? Has something happened to Hilda Semple?"

"She's dead," Quentin told him bluntly.

Van Cleff's jaw sagged and he croaked, "Oh, my God!" in a tone of utter despair. His face grew sicker as the full import of the disaster struck him. It was unthinkable. Two murders at the Met within a matter of days.

Quentin glanced at Elsa. "Can you go on with the performance?"

"I—I think so."

He looked at Van Cleff. "Have you got an understudy?"

The general manager nodded bleakly.

"Then pull yourself together and get her on the ball. Is there an empty dressing room for Miss Vaughn?"

"Next door." His voice was a squeak.

"I'll help you move," Quentin told Elsa, gathering up her costumes. She had weathered the storm rather well, he thought. Her nerves were taut, naturally, but on the whole she had herself under respectable control. He closed the door behind him and got her installed in the adjoining dressing room.

Outside, Van Cleff was nervously passing directives to his various assistants. Alone, Elsa dropped her face in her arms. Poor Hilda! From now on her roles would be passive. Impervious and uncomplaining, she would submit to the indignities of a medical examiner. She would be viewed, photographed, handled, and carted away by utter strangers. It was a distressing picture. Elsa looked up at her own white face in the mirror. Who could hate her so much? What was happening here at the Met?

First a tenor whose career had ended.

And now a soprano whose career had just begun.

CHAPTER TWENTY-ONE

The second and third acts of *Tristan und Isolde* as sung that afternoon were barely adequate. Whatever else may be said about opera singers, they are not insensitive, and no member of the cast had been left unaffected by the death of Hilda Semple. It was not a distinguished performance. Anyone with a critical ear could detect errors in phrasing and pitch which, under the circumstances, were only natural.

Karl Ecker's Tristan was somewhat on the ragged side. Elsa, however, couldn't fail to notice new and unplumbed depths to his interpretation. Tristan was a man torn between love and honor, and Ecker really suffered with him. But this new emotion was accompanied by a loss of authority; he failed to attack his high notes with assurance.

The role of Brangäne was taken by Miss Peg McAfee, winner in last year's Metropolitan Auditions of the Air. In spite of her unmistakable Hibernian origins, her Teutonic diction was quite creditable. She started off shakily but gained confidence as the opera proceeded.

As for Elsa, her performance was for the most part mechanical, except in the closing scene of the last act. Here the music took over, and she was carried away by the "Liebestod" with its rising crescendo of bitter-sweet dissonances.

It was this aria that sparked an outburst of applause. But neither Elsa nor anyone else was in a mood to acknowledge the bravos and after two curtain calls the house lights dimmed. Elsa reached her dressing room before the mass exodus had begun.

A drawn and haggard Howard Stark was waiting for her. "Elsa! Thank God you're all right! We're leaving town at once. Tonight. This thing is getting too close and we can't risk staying here."

"Where can we go?"

"Anywhere. First to your apartment to pack and then—"

"But, Howard, our contract calls for three more performances..."

"If you're alive to give them! Van Cleff understands. He'll release you."

She shook her head and sank wearily into a chair. "No, Howard, I can't run away. It's such a cowardly thing to do."

His eyes appealed eloquently to heaven. "Dear God, why did You make women so stubborn?" He confronted her ominously. "Are you blind, Elsa? Can't you understand? That bullet was addressed to you. It got misdelivered, that's all. How long do you think your luck can hold out? Stay here in New York and you're living on borrowed time.

"Besides, you can use a vacation. If you want, I'll line up a tour in South America." His palm went up, traffic cop fashion, to forestall objections. "A couple of thousand miles, that's what we want—some distance between you and this homicidal maniac. If he dares follow us that far at least we'll know who he is. We won't be walking in the dark, giving him a chance to strike at will."

Elsa stared at the far wall, kneading her fingers. "I can't run away, Howard. I have to stay."

"But why?" His voice went shrill from frustration. "What is this compulsion? What are you trying to prove? That you're brave? Okay, it's settled, you're brave. But there's a time for courage and a time for caution. I'm your business manager. You pay me for advice. Then take it, dammit, and let's get out of here!"

There were shadows under her eyes as she shook her head. "I won't renege on my contract."

"But I've already spoken to Van Cleff and he agrees."

"You had no right to do that, Howard."

His mouth tightened. "I think I did. Ten years of loyalty and devotion gave it to me. You..." his voice suddenly faltered, "you should be able to guess how I feel about you."

She leaned toward him and her face softened. "How do you feel, Howard?"

He growled brusquely, "I'm in love."

"You never said anything."

"Nor would I now. You think it's easy for me, a middle-aged bachelor, to declare himself? After all, I'm only an obscure businessman and you're an artist famous all over the world."

"Does that make any difference?" she asked softly.

"Perhaps not." Warm blood moved into his face. "Basically you're only a woman and I'm only a man."

She looked at him fondly. "Howard, I—"

"Not now." He met her words with a gruff gesture. "We have another decision to make first. It's no longer a matter of ragweed pollen and ground glass. It's a matter of life and death. We're up against a killer who means business. He won't always blunder, nor will your luck hold out forever. The law of averages is against it."

His chin jutted out. "Do you know why Van Cleff is willing to release you? For one reason only. To make sure that you'll be available next season. By then you'll be safe. The case should be solved."

---

* Helen Traubel married her business manager, William L. Bass, in 1938.

"But, Howard, subscriptions have been bought and paid for on the basis of announced programs. Every artist owes the public an obligation. The public made me what I am."

"You made yourself."

"Then I owe them something for their support."

"Not your life!" He stabbed a finger at her, emphasizing his words. "And that's what this stubbornness is liable to cost you."

Logic failed to budge her. His arguments glanced off without effect. She simply shook her head. Stark exhaled in weary resignation.

"If that's your decision, okay. What are your plans?"

"Plans?"

"For evading death. You can't just sit around and wait. You've got to take steps. My suggestion is strategic withdrawal. You've vetoed that. Okay. The next best thing is to erect some defenses."

She looked helpless. "How?"

He met her eyes squarely. "By keeping me constantly at your side, night and day."

"Howard!" She feigned outrage. "What would people say?"

"Who cares? After all, you have a choice. Which is it to be, a corpse with a stainless reputation or a prima donna slightly tarnished by gossip? The election is yours." He paused and his face reddened. "Unless you're willing to get married."

Elsa's suddenly heightened color matched his own.

"We can motor up to Greenwich," he said, reaching for her hand, waiting and holding his breath.

Elsa was quietly thoughtful. "Marriage is something I want to concentrate on, Howard. Perhaps when this thing blows over and we can see things in a clearer perspective…"

"All right." He stood up stiffly. "Whatever you say." There was an injured expression on his face. "I'm only a businessman. I can't compete with opera singers and murderers. Get dressed and I'll take you home."

CHAPTER TWENTY-TWO

No one in the backstage area had been permitted to leave. All exits were guarded. It was a little like a police convention. When the curtain fell on the last act, Karl Ecker worked his way through the jabbering throng and proceeded straight to his dressing room. His feet were heavy and leaden. Deep lines were etched around his mouth. His face showed the strain of singing an exacting role under highly abnormal conditions. The strain was in his voice, too, when he opened the door and saw his visitor.

"You again," he said.

The churlishness of his tone stung her. Edwina DeBrett looked oddly bruised. She sat on the divan, her eyes restless and the skin stretched taut across the bones of her face. She was jittery and nervous as he crossed over and stood in front of her.

"Your lack of discretion grows, Edwina. Must you run to my dressing room every time I perform?"

"Where else? The whole backstage area is sealed off. There's nothing wrong with a DeBrett visiting a star's dressing room to congratulate him, is there?"

He turned sullenly and sat down at the dressing table, and

rested his forehead in the palm of his hand. Edwina watched him and finally broke the silence.

"This hits you rather hard, doesn't it, Karl? You were really fond of her."

"Who?" His voice was dull.

"Hilda Semple."

He looked up, his eyes glazed.

"I know you've been seeing a lot of each other."

A sudden muscle twitched in his jaw. "Have you been spying on me, Edwina?"

"Not at all. People gossip and I've seen you around."

He did not move or speak. He just kept staring at her emptily. Then he shrugged listlessly. "Well, it makes no difference now. She's dead now."

In a slow precise voice Edwina said, "You never should have cheated on me, Karl."

His manner changed. Quick anger brought him to his feet. Red veins sprouted through his face and his huge fists were lumped at his sides. "What are you trying to build?" he said harshly. "I never gave you an exclusive. We signed no contract. You're no child. You went into this thing with your eyes open."

He paused while his eyes narrowed in cold speculation. "So you were jealous of Hilda. That opens new vistas. Tell me, Edwina, were you jealous enough to follow her into Elsa's dressing room and—"

She arched her back like a cat and called him a name. Her teeth gleamed between her lips. "Don't try to throw it off on me, Karl. Maybe you were trying to get rid of her."

He laughed nastily. "If all my women were like you I'd probably have to commit murder to get rid of them."

She caught her breath. Then she smiled stiffly. "My God, what's happening to us, Karl? Is this the best performance we can manage in an emergency?"

He sat down and shook his head remorsefully. "Sorry, Edwina. I'm not myself. None of us are. All this violence and killing..." He gestured helplessly.

She kept her voice low. "I think we had better stay friends, Karl. You see, I'm in a bit of trouble and it involves you."

"Me?" Thick brows descended over his frowning eyes.

"I never told you this. I didn't want you to worry about it. But in spite of all our caution, your friend Rudolf Salz found out about us. He came to me several weeks ago and demanded money. A loan, he called it. There were no threats, just a hint that my husband might be interested."

Ecker got quickly to his feet. "What did you do?"

"What could I do? I gave him a check for five thousand dollars."

He dug his fingers into her shoulders cruelly.

"Don't, Karl! You're hurting me! They only know that I gave him the money, not why I gave it to him."

His breathing was uneven. "Who told them?"

"Lieutenant Quentin found my canceled check."

A vein bulged in a blue diagonal across his temple. "You little fool! Why didn't you pay him in cash?"

"It never occurred to me. Nor to Salz, I suppose. Neither of us were old hands at blackmail."

"Then you should have had sense enough to destroy the check."

She shrugged fatalistically. "Well, I didn't, and there's no use crying over spilt milk."

Ecker was almost blind with controlled rage. "Do you know what it could mean—a scandal like that?"

"Yes. It could mean a divorce."

"Divorce!" he cried in a tone of concentrated ferocity. "Is that all you can think of? What about my career? An ugly divorce suit could ruin it. That must not happen, Edwina!"

His anger hadn't touched her at all. She seemed imperturbably amused. "Why should it, Karl? I'll never tell anyone."

A single knock sounded against the door. Ecker swung around, composed his face with an effort, and said, "Come in."

The door opened. Lieutenant Quentin stood on the threshold. He carried an automatic pistol hanging from a pencil stuck through its trigger guard. He spoke in a flat voice, without inflection.

"One of my men found this gun behind some old flat-drops.[*] It has recently been fired. Do you recognize it, Mr. Ecker?"

The tenor looked surprised. "Why—it looks familiar."

"It should. It's your gun, registered in your name."

Edwina gasped. Ecker's mouth fell open in consternation.

"We haven't tested it yet," Quentin said, "but we're pretty sure this is the gun that killed Hilda Semple."

A micrometer check of the barrel rifling would have to wait until the M.E. recovered the slug, but his experienced eye had diagnosed the wound as the result of a thirty-two, which was the caliber of the weapon in his hand. He saw Ecker swallow painfully.

"May I see the gun, please?"

"Not now. We're saving it for prints." In all his years on the force Quentin had never yet found an identifiable set of fingerprints on a hand weapon,[†] but he was taking no chances and overlooking no bets.

Ecker spread his hands. "If that is really my gun, then it must be the one that was stolen from my apartment several days ago."

A humorless smile barely moved Quentin's lips.

"Not good enough, Mr. Ecker. I'm afraid it won't wash."

---

[*] A "flat" is a flat piece of scenery, usually painted on canvas, on a frame, often stored in the theater wings.

[†] This is because the grip of the weapon is often textured; smooth surfaces produce better prints.

"I mean it." Ecker was leaning forward earnestly. "The gun was taken from my desk. I even went down to the precinct station and reported it. It's all there in the records. They made me sign some forms."

Quentin sighed. Finding and identifying the gun had narrowed it down. Now everybody was back in again.

"How long did you have the gun?" he asked.

"About a year. I got it after… after what happened to my wife."

"You kept it in a desk drawer."

"Yes."

"Who had access?"

"Most anybody. I entertain a lot."

Quentin swallowed his disappointment. "Where did you buy it?"

"I didn't. I borrowed it from my brother-in-law, Stanley DeBrett."

"Have you any idea who might have taken the gun?"

"No, sir." Ecker seemed offended. "Most of my friends are artists, musicians, painters, writers, high in society—people who do not go around killing."

For once Quentin lost his manners. He made an ugly sound. "Save that for someone else," he said unpleasantly. "I'm in the business. I know what kind of people kill and for what." He paused reflectively. "You were a friend of Hilda Semple's?"

"Yes."

"How close?"

Ecker shrugged. "We sang together in a number of operas."

"Isn't it a fact that you were a little more than mere friends?"

Ecker looked at him, his face bland and innocent.

"Don't bother denying it," Quentin went on. "She was a frequent visitor to your apartment and vice versa. We know that to be a fact. I've had a man following her ever since Rudolf Salz was killed and we learned about their contract."

Ecker blinked at him. "You don't think Hilda stole my gun?"

"No, that's fairly obvious." Quentin shook his head. Through a corner of one eye he was watching Edwina. "I had something else in mind. A man like you, with your talent, your looks, your fame, would certainly have more than one admirer." He paused significantly. "Women make jealous rivals. I happened to be in the corridor outside long enough to hear some of your dialogue with Mrs. DeBrett here." He gave his words a chance to sink in. "It's something to think about, isn't it?"

Edwina stood motionless. Her body narrowed and seemed to shrink into itself. Quentin's intent must have been obvious. He was throwing a little more fat into the fire, hoping to start a blaze. But he kept silent. Suddenly Quentin looked directly at her.

"How long have you been backstage, Mrs. DeBrett?"

"Since the first-act curtain."

"Then you were here when Hilda Semple was killed?"

"Obviously. Since there were witnesses I won't deny it."

"Who came with you?"

"My husband and stepdaughter. We separated backstage."

His eyes were disconcertingly steady. "From what I heard through the door, I would say that you too had access to the gun."

She did not answer. Her face had lost its youthful look and seemed colorless. Abruptly Quentin pulled the door open again. "Stay available, both of you," he said, and left.

Edwina DeBrett and Karl Ecker stood staring at each other. Then Ecker walked to the door and peered into the corridor. Apparently satisfied, he came back. His expression was curiously strained, but his voice was soft.

"You *were* in my apartment the day before I missed the gun, Edwina. Did you take it?"

The years were merciless now. Her feature were gaunt and angular. "Don't say that, Karl. Don't even think it."

"I hope you're telling the truth, *Liebchen*. That detective is a very smart man. He could build up a good case against you, not only for the death of Hilda, but for the death of Rudolf Salz, too."

"You're crazy."

"Hilda because of jealousy; Salz because he threatened your security."

The expression of utter revulsion on Edwina's face was proof that certain emotions are stronger than love, or whatever it was she felt for Karl Ecker. She looked at him for a moment, then straightened with a semblance of dignity, and walked from the room.

CHAPTER TWENTY-THREE

The murder of Hilda Semple, so soon after the demise of Rudolf Salz, set off a journalistic explosion heard all around the country. A.P., U.P., and I.N.S. cleared their wires for a special bulletin. Newspapers carried the story under banner headlines. *Life* magazine prepared a picture history of the Metropolitan during the golden years of Gatti-Casazza and Otto Kahn.* *Look* prepared a biographical sketch of the dead soprano as a little girl. And the *Daily Worker*, quite unaccountably, pointed out the weakness of capitalistic opera by running a story on Feodor Chaliapin.

On top of all this Lieutenant Sam Quentin had a hunch which struck pay dirt. The gun found backstage was checked against the bullet that had killed Ivy Ecker a year ago. Bullet and barrel riflings matched. And since the gun at that time was admittedly in Stanley DeBrett's possession, he was again taken into custody. The charge was a grave one, and no lawyer had been able to spring

---

* Giulio Gatti-Cassaza was the manager of the Met from 1908 until his retirement in 1935 (he had managed La Scala in Milan from 1898 to 1908). Kahn (1867–1934) was a very wealthy financier, philanthropist, and artistic patron who served for many years as president and chairman of the board of the Met (as well as vice president of the New York Philharmonic Orchestra).

him on a writ. Beyond a flat denial of guilt, the authorities found that he had lost the use of his tongue.

The situation at the Met, of course, was intolerable. If things continued like this the whole company might be wiped out. And so the top brass of the city's law-enforcement agencies took a hand. By nightfall of that same day, Saturday, ranking municipal employees gathered together for a conference in the office of Inspector Nicholas Patrick. The Commissioner himself sat in. So did District Attorney Alden Willard, with his assistant, Mark Simon. Lieutenant Sam Quentin made himself inconspicuous at the back of the room.

The only outsider who unquestionably had an interest in the meeting was Elsa Vaughn, and she had been asked to attend while they mapped out a campaign designed to keep her alive.

District Attorney Alden Willard was tall, iron-haired, and suave. The rimless glasses pinched against his nose were polished to a high luster. He was treating Elsa Vaughn with all the deference and respect usually accorded to important citizens by elected officials.

"Then it's understood, Miss Vaughn," he said crisply. "You agree. You will be under guard until this case is solved. Three plain-clothes men will work around the clock. When you leave your apartment one of them will never be more than ten paces behind you."

She smiled wanly. "If anything happens to me, at least you'll catch the villain."

"Nothing is going to happen," he assured her. "All murderers are convinced they can get away with the deed. If they thought otherwise they wouldn't commit it. We'll publish the fact that you're under guard. Our killer will have to lay low or get nabbed. As a matter of fact, we mean business and we'll catch him anyway."

"You say 'him.' Are you sure it's a man?"

"The pronoun is merely a convenience. The killer may be a woman." He cleared his throat impressively. "Now, Miss Vaughn, I know we've been over all this ground before, but I want you to go back, dig in, please, search your memory. Can you think of anyone at all who might gain by your death?"

She gestured helplessly. "At one time, Hilda Semple."

"But no longer. Not since she became a victim. Anyone else?"

She shook her head. "I'm afraid not."

He looked at Quentin. "How about you, Lieutenant? You've been in this from the start. What do you think?"

"We're still trying to line it up, sir."

"Ivy Ecker and Hilda Semple were both shot by the same gun. Outside of that fact, do you believe there is any connection between the two deaths?"

"It's a possibility. At the moment, however, I can't see any link."

"Let's find one," the D.A. said firmly. "That's what we're here for. Stanley DeBrett, for example. As owner of the gun that killed Ivy Ecker, with access to the same weapon after he gave it to his brother-in-law, he also had the means and opportunity for killing Miss Semple, since he was backstage at the time."

"But no motive."

"No motive for killing Miss Semple. That's right." He nodded vigorously and pointed a finger. "But how about Miss Vaughn? We're agreed that she was the intended victim."

Elsa broke in, looking incredulous. "You mean Stanley DeBrett tried to kill me? Oh, no! I'll never believe that. What earthly reason could he possibly have?"

"Perhaps you know something vital to his safety."

"But I don't." She shook her head emphatically.

Willard smiled thinly. "You may think you don't. The chances are you're not aware of the fact. Its true significance may have escaped you."

She looked skeptical.

"We can afford to overlook no possibilities," Willard said. "Think, Miss Vaughn, think hard. Do you have any knowledge, any secret, any fragment of information which might expose someone to serious danger?"

Her eyes were puckered in concentration. She was aware of something at the back of her mind, an idea, just beyond her grasp, as elusive as a handful of smoke. But too much had happened today and her brain was not functioning with any degree of clarity. She shook her head.

"How about your manager, Howard Stark?" Willard asked.

Elsa answered very quickly. "All right, what about him?"

"I understand that he controls your finances."

"Yes, he does." Her fingers were tightly clenched.

"A man can be tempted by large sums of money."

"I trust Howard implicitly."

"Do you? Well, it's no secret that he's in a hole financially. Your own publicity man, Dave Lang, found out that Stark invested for you in an almost defunct football club, earning a handsome commission for himself. Is that why you trust him?"

She replied defiantly. "I know all about that. As a matter of fact, Howard advised me against the deal, but I insisted. There were certain reasons, personal and sentimental, why I wanted that stock."

Willard was a little surprised at the sudden steel in her manner and he backtracked. "All right, we'll leave it for now. I'm not so sure—" He turned to glare as the door opened and a thin-nosed man with protruding eyes put his head through.

"What is it, Fisher?" he demanded.

The man obviously was holding himself in. A charge of excitement gleamed in his eyes. He stepped into the room and proffered a chamois bag to the District Attorney.

"Something I found in the garage in Stanley DeBrett's place up in Ridgefield. Mark Simon sent me there."

Willard fingered the bag and peered in. What he saw seemed to electrify him. He looked up sharply. "Where in the garage?"

"Under a plank on the second floor."

Willard slapped his thigh smartly. "Got him!" It was a crow of triumph. "Gentlemen, Stanley DeBrett is cooked. We've nailed him now and we've nailed him good. Look here."

He upended the bag over Inspector Patrick's desk. A pile of jewelry cascaded out, flashing at them with green, red, and white fire.

"Ivy Ecker's jewelry!" Mark Simon could not repress his elation. "My hunch worked out, chief. We've got him now, signed, sealed, and delivered. DeBrett was my candidate from the start. Let's see him wriggle off the hook this time."

Inspector Patrick was convinced. "I guess that's it. The jewels in conjunction with the gun should do it. He's cooked, all right."

But Lieutenant Sam Quentin was scowling. "I don't know. Suppose it does clear up the Ecker case—what about Rudolf Salz and Hilda Semple? Can we pin those on DeBrett, too? Will the newspapers let up because we've solved a year-old murder case? We've still got a job on our hands. What's the big celebration for?"

It dampened their spirits, but only momentarily. Willard rubbed his palms. "With Stanley DeBrett under lock and key, nothing is going to happen. However, we'll keep Miss Vaughn under surveillance as an added precaution." He turned briskly toward his assistant. "We've got work to do, Mark, a case to prepare for the Grand Jury."

He gave Elsa a courtly bow and marched from the room with Mark Simon at his heels. Elsa kept her blurred gaze on the pile of jewels in a kind of dazed fascination. Sickness lurched through her again. Her head was no good; it refused to function. The idea of Stanley DeBrett's guilt was too unspeakably dreadful.

Sam Quentin emerged grim-faced from his preoccupation. He went to the door and crooked a finger. Sergeant Cullen appeared.

"I want you to drive Miss Vaughn home, Sergeant. Stick with her until I select a detail to relieve you. Understand?"

"Yes, sir."

He stood politely aside and let Elsa precede him through the door.

CHAPTER TWENTY-FOUR

Stanley DeBrett sat on a cot in his cell. The fine new city prison offered aesthetic cleanliness but no comfort. His eyes were blankly fixed on a barred aperture in the wall which framed a bleak view of New York's skyline. He might have been in a state of suspended animation. For almost an hour he had been sitting with no muscular reflexes beyond those required by minimum respiration. Nor did he evince any interest at the sound of a key turning in the lock, and only when a voice spoke his name did his eyes shift their focus.

The Rt. Hon. Alden Willard, District Attorney of New York County, was in his cell, wearing an expression of unutterable smugness.

In a voice that was firm but not loud, DeBrett said, "I was allowed one call. I phoned a lawyer. He promised to come right down. Where is he?"

"Later, Mr. DeBrett. First I want to—"

"No. Is this the Middle Ages? Am I being held incommunicado? It was my impression that the processes of a democracy—"

"Slow down, Mr. DeBrett. Your lawyer is on the job. I've spoken to him. The fact is, his hands are tied. There's nothing he can do at the present time. We have every right to hold you for questioning as a material witness. This is a murder case and it calls for an entirely new set of rules. I was elected by the people to do a specific job and I mean to do it. You have refused to talk and you have offered no explanation. If that refusal is due to guilt, then I'm wasting my time. If not, then you're acting childishly. And if it's because you're protecting someone, that makes you an accessory after the fact. Even your own lawyer would advise you to talk."

"Then let him do so."

"In good time. I expect to go before the Grand Jury tomorrow morning. Perhaps if you opened up we could avoid unpleasant complications. If not, I guarantee you'll be indicted."

"On the basis of a gun that once belonged to me?" DeBrett snorted. "Nonsense!"

"Your sister was killed by that gun, Mr. DeBrett."

"If your ballistics men say so, I have to believe it. However, I didn't pull the trigger."

"Every accused pleads innocence, Mr. DeBrett. The jury doesn't have to believe him."

"Perhaps not, but they like to be shown a motive."

"Which we can do, sir. I've been practicing law for twenty years and I think it will prove an adequate one. Your sister charged you with mismanagement of her estate. She threatened to sue you and ruin your reputation."

DeBrett was staring hard at the District Attorney. "Where did you learn that?"

"It was overheard by a member of your household."

"My wife told you?"

"Never mind. We know where to get a pipeline when we need it. The story is true, isn't it?"

"My sister was mistaken."

"That may be. But she didn't know it—and a lawsuit would have been embarrassing."

"Not embarrassing enough for me to commit murder."

"That question will be decided by a jury. It's your denial against concrete evidence."

"Evidence of what?"

"The murder weapon, a gun that was admittedly in your possession at the time she was killed."

DeBrett scoffed. "Which anyone could have taken from my home and later replaced."

"Taken by whom?" Willard was regarding him with a flinty stare. "By your daughter? By your wife?"

The broker's face congealed and he sat in silence.

"Have I touched a sore spot, Mr. DeBrett?"

His face was empty. "You're fishing. You're floundering around in a swamp. You have nothing but circumstantial evidence. You can never convict me on the basis of a gun and a family quarrel."

"We don't have to." The District Attorney was unpleasantly smug. "We have other evidence, and a lot more damning than the gun."

"Is that so?" DeBrett was coolly skeptical. "For example?"

"The jewelry stolen at the time your sister was killed."

DeBrett waved it carelessly aside. "I was under the impression Albert Barbizon cleared me on that. He gave you proof where I got the pin."

"The pin, yes." Willard paused, savoring the moment. "But not the rest of it."

DeBrett looked at him. His brows came together in a sharp frown. "What do you mean?"

"Your family heirlooms." Willard's voice turned acid and challenging. "The whole booty, all the rest of it. Found under a plank where you hid it in your garage up in Ridgefield."

Stanley DeBrett stopped breathing.

The District Attorney moved closer, jaw thrust out. "That hits home, doesn't it? One of our men drove up for a look around. He found it there. The stuff is at police Headquarters now, ready to be used as evidence."

For a moment DeBrett's guard was down and he looked vulnerable. Then his face settled into a hard mask. He said, "You went up—you searched my place without a warrant?"

"Yes, sir." Willard was complacent. "Strictly speaking, it was illegal. I admit that we stepped over the line and I'll cross that bridge when we come to it. The point is, we got results. Pull up a chair, Mr. DeBrett, and sit down with the jury. Look at the facts now. I don't say you stole those jewels for their intrinsic value. Your purpose was to confuse the motive, to make it look like burglary. But the bald fact remains that Ivy was killed with your gun, and that the jewels were subsequently found in your garage. How do you like it? What verdict do you think a jury would return?"

Stanley DeBrett did not like it. His composure was shaken and his face was strained. A muscle twitched under his eye.

Suddenly he sat forward. "One moment. Consider this, Mr. Willard...would I hang on to that gun if I had used it? Would I hide the jewels in a place they were bound to be found if I ever came under suspicion? Give me credit for some intelligence! I'm not a complete imbecile."

Willard nodded. "I realize that. But I'm also taking into consideration the fact that murderers make mistakes. That's why they're caught. I admit we're late on this one; we should have checked your gun a year ago, but we missed the boat there. Which was only natural because at the time it looked like an open and shut case, burglary and homicide. You were her brother, eminent, well known, a respected citizen. We had no earthly reason to suspect you. So we're late. But there is no Statute of Limitations in a murder case."

He paused. His gaze was direct. "Maybe you are innocent. That remains to be seen. As things now stand, I can build a mighty convincing case." He leveled a finger. "Unless you can prove you were framed. Is there anything you'd like to say about that, Mr. DeBrett?"

"Such as?"

The District Attorney shrugged. "Well, you might have some theories about your wife."

DeBrett sat back. He did not speak; his face was carved out of stone.

Willard leaned forward. "I'm not firing in the dark. I've been over the ground thoroughly with Lieutenant Quentin. Your wife had a motive for killing Salz. The man was blackmailing her. And she had access to the gun on both occasions. First, when it was in your possession and Ivy was killed; second, when it was in Ecker's possession and Hilda Semple was killed. We can dig up a motive there, too. Jealousy. The fact that Semple was killed in Elsa Vaughn's dressing room doesn't necessarily mean it was a mistake. She could have been deliberately followed there and shot. And another thing—your wife undoubtedly has a key to the property in Ridgefield. She could easily have gone up there and planted the jewels. If things turned out right it could mean your conviction for murder. She would have her freedom and at least one-third of your fortune."

DeBrett looked up. His face was gray and beads of moisture laced his upper lip. His brow was a network of wrinkles as the wheels turned in his head.

Willard plunged on, excited by his own line of reasoning. He was beginning to convince himself. He said, "I think she'd be willing to stand by and let you take the rap—maybe even help out with a little push. But we have no evidence against her and we'll get none if she decides to keep sitting on it." He paused, his eyes glowing. "Are you willing to help us, Mr. DeBrett?"

The broker swallowed. "How?"

"By building a fire under her. Little hints along the angles I've outlined. If she's guilty, she'll backtrack, looking for mistakes, trying to cover, and that's where a lot of them trip up."

He watched DeBrett eagerly. The broker's mouth was a tight ring of indecision. Then he said, "Let me get something straight, Mr. Willard. Everything you said at first, about me, about the gun, about my sister's jewelry—you mean you don't believe any of it?"

The D.A. shrugged expressively. "Suppose I put it this way. We can make out a case against you, a powerful case, but I'm ready to admit there are holes. A smart lawyer could raise doubts in a jury's mind. Conceivably he might squeeze you through. The whole state is watching this case and I can't afford to climb out on a limb. I want to cover every possible angle."

"Will you arrange to release me?"

"Yes."

DeBrett nodded promptly. "All right. What do you want me to do?"

CHAPTER TWENTY-FIVE

"But you're a lawyer," Jane said into the telephone, her voice shrill with anxiety. "There must be something you can do! Of course Dad isn't guilty. It's fantastic. It's a plot of some kind and they're all in on it. Just get him out. I don't care how—that's your business. Because if you don't—"

The earpiece started to buzz and she listened. She looked miserable and woebegone. Her shoulders drooped as she got a brief lecture on evidence and material witnesses and obstructing justice. "All right," she said numbly. "Do whatever you can."

She hung up, feeling small and alone. She had tried to reach Elsa, but the line went unanswered. Howard Stark was nowhere to be found. Edwina had disappeared shortly after the arrest. The whole world seemed hostile, an implacable enemy. At first the news of her father's arrest left her in a state of shock. Then came a feeling of burning anger at the law's stupidity. Now she was listless, apathetic.

She gave a start as the doorbell rang, and her fists clenched involuntarily. If those reporters were back...

She went to the door and opened it. Instantly her spirits leaped. Jane could not remember when the sight of anyone had been so welcome.

Dave Lang stood on the threshold, tentatively searching her face.

"Oh, Dave…" Her voice choked.

He came in quickly and put his arms around her, holding her close. She buried her face against his shoulder and sobbed quietly for a moment. He spoke to her, commiserating in low sympathetic tones.

"Everything's going to be all right now, baby, you'll see."

She looked up at last. "I'm so glad you came, Dave."

He could have kissed her then, but he resisted the impulse and said, "There's no time to be lost, baby. We've got work to do."

Hope dawned in her eyes. She watched him expectantly.

"I've been thinking," he said. "There are only two ways to look at it. Either your dad is guilty or he's innocent."

"No." Her voice was suddenly fierce. "There's only one way to look at it. He's innocent."

"Okay. We'll proceed on that premise. It means he's been framed and we'll have to prove it."

"But how?"

"Well, it's a year since your aunt was killed. Evidence in a murder case cools off mighty fast. My suggestion is this: let's take a run up to the house at Ridgefield. I believe the jewels were planted there recently, after the gun was identified, to help clinch the case against your father. We can nose around, talk to the neighbors. One of them may have seen somebody at the house. A description would give us a lead. What do you say?"

Her answer was an eager flurry of action as she whirled toward a hall closet. She faced him, shrugging into a light blue coat. There were signs of life in her eyes and some of the color was back in her cheeks. This was much better than sitting dismally back and waiting for developments.

Dave had his car out front. He climbed in after her and slid behind the wheel. The engine caught at once in a thunder of combustion. He headed up the West Side Highway and the Sawmill, slanting off toward Connecticut on the Cross County Parkway. Jane sat beside him in silent preoccupation. Guardrails hissed past. Autumn was late this year and foliage burned redly along the sides of the road. The hills unrolled like a painting on canvas as Dave's foot bore down on the accelerator. He could see her face through the rear-vision mirror and he promised himself that they would take this drive again when she would be free to concentrate on her escort.

"Jane?"

"Yes."

"Tell me, who hates your father?"

"Hates him?" She was startled. "Nobody. Why?"

"Because only a ruthless and implacable enemy would deliberately steer a man into so much trouble. I've heard some talk about your stepmother."

"Edwina?" Her eyes flickered. "Edwina doesn't love Dad. She never has. But I want to be fair and I can't say that she actually hates him."

"Do you get along well with her?"

"Not very well. In a way, I suppose it's partly my fault. I couldn't imagine anyone taking Mother's place. I resented it when Dad got married again and brought Edwina home. I realize now how unfair that was. Dad was lonely. He needed someone. Edwina may not have been the right woman, but it wouldn't have made any difference. I was cold and hostile. And then, later, when I tried to be friendly, it was too late. She ignored me. Edwina's very good at that. I was merely something around the house that had to be tolerated."

"Do you think she married your father for his money?"

"I'm sure of it."

"Do you know the contents of his will?"

"No, of course not. We never discuss money, but I assume he's leaving everything to me."

"Not everything," Dave said. "The law doesn't permit a man to disinherit his own wife.* She'd be entitled to at least a third."

Jane shrugged indifferently.

Dave said, "People have killed for money without hating. Edwina had plenty to gain by easing your father out of the picture. Seems a little diabolical. The point is, could she be so heartless?"

Jane was peering through the windshield. Twilight was painting dusty shadows across the land as the sun slipped down behind the treetops. Dave switched his headlamps on; it was growing dark fast.

"Better slow down," Jane said. "We turn left at the next crossing."

He saw it and decelerated, swinging the car around. A mile later, in second gear, they were winding up a steep grade. Naked-limbed trees slipped past them like gaunt sentinels in the dusk. The moon was pale and motionless against the lowering sky.

"Those two gateposts," Jane said.

Pebbles spun crunchingly away from the tires as they rolled toward a large, comfortable-looking house with a wide veranda facing the silent foothills.

Dave parked, climbed out after Jane, and followed her onto the porch. She fumbled in her purse for a key. A large square room, opening off the entrance, sprang into view when she flipped the switch. It was warm and homelike with walls of knotty pine and furniture of Colonial vintage.

They stopped short and exchanged quick, startled looks.

---

* This is a complex law known as "dower." It was repealed in 1930 in New York, with certain provisions retained for those married before 1930. Because the DeBretts likely married after that date, this statement is probably completely inaccurate. Such a rule should not be confused with the intestacy laws that leave a substantial portion of an estate to a surviving spouse in cases where the decedent has no will.

They were not alone. From the rear of the house a light glowed dimly. The smell of freshly brewing coffee was strong. Jane caught Dave's sleeve in an involuntary gesture of apprehension.

He signaled for silence. His eyes searched the room for a weapon. He crossed to the fireplace and firmly grasped the iron poker. Thus armed, he headed toward the kitchen. No boards creaked under his cautious footsteps.

It was an immaculately white room. Blue flames on an immense gas range licked at the bottom of a coffeepot. The liquid bubbled energetically. With the poker brandished in his fist, Dave felt a little silly and overdramatic. The room was empty.

Jane was at his heels and he whispered, "I think we'd better tour the house."

It was in a bedroom at the rear that Jane suddenly clutched his arm and pointed through the window.

"Look, Dave—the garage."

He saw a light burning on the second floor of a building some fifty yards back.

"Stay here," he ordered.

"No. I'm going with you."

"There may be fireworks and I don't want you underfoot."

But she shook her head and trailed stubbornly along. In a way, he couldn't blame her, and he knew better than to argue with a determined female. A back door led out onto the lawn. They moved quietly toward the garage. A soft wind rustled tree branches, and crisp leaves parachuted slowly down in the moonlight.

The silhouette of a dark sedan was dimly visible through the open doors. Dave touched the hood. It was warm and the engine was still pinking.* He gripped the poker and headed for a narrow stairway, with Jane close behind.

---

* The "pink, pink" sound of an engine cooling off.

Anemic light shone through a doorway at the head of the landing. Living quarters for a chauffeur. Dave stood immobile at the sound of a shuffling footstep within. Jane's breath came rapidly. Two more steps brought a sparsely furnished room into view.

A wide plank had been removed from the center of the floor. Hunched over the gaping hole, peering into it, was a woman.

"Looking for something?" Dave asked.

She whirled, crouching back, her eyes round and wild. Her palms flew to her throat.

"Who are you?" she whispered.

"A friend of mine," Jane said, showing herself.

Edwina DeBrett let her breath out with inexpressible relief. She shuddered and gave a small shaken laugh.

"Jane!" Her composure was returning. "You frightened me. What are you doing here?"

"I might ask you the same question." Jane's voice was cold and impersonal.

Dave said, "She's right, Mrs. DeBrett. I doubt if the police are finished up here yet. They'll want to take fingerprints of the whole garage and by now you've probably gummed things up."

She met his steady regard coolly. "Do I know you?"

"The name is Dave Lang. You haven't answered the question."

She shrugged carelessly. "I couldn't face anyone in town. All that malicious gossip and those reporters. I had to get away and this was the only place I could think of."

Jane was scornful. "So you left Dad as soon as he was in trouble."

Edwina smiled at her indulgently. "But, darling, I'm no lawyer. How could I help?"

Jane's lip curled. "You must love him very much."

Edwina said coolly, "Now, Jane, let's not have a scene in front of strangers."

"He's not the stranger." Jane sounded bitter. "I've known him only a few days and he's less of a stranger than you are."

It warmed Dave to hear her say so, but this was no time to draw up a bill of indictment, and he intervened quickly.

"Recriminations will get us nowhere," he said. "We drove up here, Mrs. DeBrett, in the hope of finding some evidence that might help clear your husband. Perhaps you can give us a hand."

She regarded him closely. "Are you a police officer, Mr. Lang?"

"No, I'm not."

"You look familiar. Haven't I seen you somewhere?"

"Around the Met. I'm associated with Elsa Vaughn—public relations."

"Oh." She smiled disarmingly. "Of course, I'll help. What do you want me to do?"

"Answer some questions. For example, was that plank off the floor when you got here, or did you move it?"

"The opening was just this way."

"Then you haven't touched anything?"

"No."

"What made you come out to the garage?"

Her shrug was guileless. "Simple curiosity. I wanted to see where the famous DeBrett heirlooms had been hidden. Was there anything wrong in that?"

"Probably not. Tell me this, Mrs. DeBrett—do you believe your husband is innocent?"

"Of course."

"Could you suggest any explanation for the evidence against him?"

She gestured helplessly. "I'm at a complete loss, Mr. Lang."

"Did you know that he owned a gun at the time Ivy was killed?"

"It was no secret. He kept it as a souvenir of the First World War."

"Any idea who might have taken it?"

"I'm afraid not."

"Is there anyone who dislikes him enough to frame him for murder?"

She considered in silence for a moment and then looked at him. "Your approach may be wrong, Mr. Lang. All this evidence may simply have been arranged as a matter of convenience, to deflect suspicion from the real culprit."

It was a good point and Dave nodded slowly. "How long are you going to stay here, Mrs. DeBrett?"

"For a day or two."

"Then we'll know where to find you." He nodded briefly and turned. "Let's go, Jane."

He knew that Jane was very angry; the aura of hostility that surrounded her was a palpable thing. Once outside, she stopped to confront him.

"Edwina fooled you, didn't she? Just as she fools all the men—so sweet and innocent and helpful. Are you blind, Dave? Can't you see it's just an act, that she's not to be trusted? She doesn't believe Dad is innocent. She doesn't care whether he's cleared or not. She—she's—" Her voice died, choked with emotion.

Dave gripped her shoulders. "Easy now. We've still got work to do. We were going to talk to some of the neighbors, remember?"

She took a breath. "I'm sorry, Dave. All right, let's try."

They made the rounds, but it was a fruitless tour. Some homes were closed for the winter. The permanent residents had seen no one near the DeBrett residence or were minding their own business. Anyone could have driven up at night, Dave realized now, and planted the jewels under cover of darkness.

Silent, discouraged, they headed toward the car, shunning the house. Traffic was light along the Parkway. It was a crisp night. The sky was cloudless and reeling with stars. A distant moon sprinkled the earth with silver. They drove in silence while the engine gulped thirstily from its fuel tank.

Jane was the first to speak. "I can't go home, Dave. I don't want to be alone with Edwina tonight."

"But Edwina's staying in Ridgefield."

"You can't believe anything she says. She may change her mind."

"All right." He nodded. "I'll take you to a hotel. Or wait—" He had a sudden inspiration. "How about Elsa? Will she put you up?"

"I guess so."

"Then I'd better call her before she goes to sleep."

Jane pointed through the windshield. "Look. Isn't that a tavern up ahead?"

Dave slowed and pulled up in front of a small red brick building with a neon sign advertising beer. "Only be a minute," he told her, and went in. The bartender changed a bill for him. He sat in the phone booth and clinked coins into the slot. The operator put him through. Elsa must have been sitting right at the instrument; a single ring and she came on.

"Hello." Her voice was too loud and too shrill.

"Dave Lang, Elsa."

"Dave!" He could sense the tension. It came over thirty miles of wire, a tangible thing between them. She was wound up tighter than the spring on a dollar watch. "Am I glad you called! If I can't talk to someone right away I'll explode. Can you hurry over? Where are you?"

He told her.

"Oh, but that's miles away." She sounded bleak. Dave caught her excitement. "What is it, Elsa? What's up?" He was holding the phone so hard his fingers ached.

Her words came out in a breathless rush. "Listen, Dave. I know what happened to Ivy. She wasn't murdered at all. And I think I know who killed Rudolf Salz and Hilda Semple. It—"

She stopped. A gasp caught at her throat. And then her voice came to him from a great distance, small and thin with shock: "You... Oh, my God...!"

The scalp under Dave's hair contracted. "Elsa!" he shouted.

But the line was dead. There was no sound. No sound at all. Frantically he jiggled the hook. His heart was whamming wildly against his ribs.

"Operator!" he croaked. "Operator, get me the New York police, quick."

CHAPTER TWENTY-SIX

Sergeant Cullen, at the wheel of a squad car carrying Elsa Vaughn as a passenger, relished his assignment. He was hoping they kept him on the job. With a bit of luck he might nab the guy responsible for all these homicides. The picture he painted for himself was very pleasant indeed—a special citation awarded by the Mayor on the steps of City Hall, with Miss Vaughn present to thank him personally. He surveyed her appreciatively through the rear-vision mirror. These Wagnerian sopranos were something special, all right.

He braked in front of Elsa's building and jumped out to give her a hand. "Got to call in, Miss Vaughn. Will I be able to use your phone?"

"Of course." Her tone was friendly, but she looked tired and abstracted.

The elevator took them up. Cullen followed her through the foyer, but he could not stop fast enough to avoid a collision. Elsa, with a sharp intake of breath, had pulled up short.

"Howard!" she cried, and then she was running.

He lay sprawled out on the living-room floor, evidently ambushed from behind. The ugly bruise behind his right ear had stopped bleeding. The weapon, a bronze statuette of Beethoven that usually rested on Elsa's piano, lay on its side near the fallen man. His face was gray and still.

Elsa went down on her knees beside him, her throat choked up with emotion. *Howard! Oh, Howard! Not you too, darling!* The sickness was overpowering and she was oblivious to the shambles surrounding him.

But the scene would have been a familiar one. She had seen it before in Rudolf Salz's apartment: the whole place upside down, records broken and strewn about in wild confusion. Only at the very perimeter of her consciousness was Elsa aware of this destruction. Her attention was on Howard. Suddenly her heart somersaulted. Relief surged through her. There was a movement in his throat, the beat of a pulse.

She whispered, "He's alive...."

Cullen had seen it too. "Is there a doctor in the building?" he demanded.

She nodded, not trusting her voice. He turned and raced out through the foyer. In the outer hall his finger held the button until the elevator came up. The operator's protest died unspoken at the sight of his face.*

"Get the doctor, boy!" Cullen snapped. "On the double. Emergency."

He left the door open. Elsa, who was still bending over Howard, turned, pleading for the reassurance. "Will he be all right?"

Cullen shrugged. "I'm no doctor, Miss Vaughn. But he's still alive and maybe we got here in time."

There was a tentative knock at the open door and then a

---

* The elevator operator, that is; in New York, until after World War II, many buildings—especially luxury housing—had manual elevators operated by a person whose job it was to sit on a stool and run the elevator, delivering the passengers to the correct floor.

short round-faced man carrying a black leather bag appeared. He trotted forward without wasting time on amenities. He got out his stethoscope and listened. He folded it and reached for Howard's wrist to clock his pulse. Elsa was watching him with fearful anxiety, but there was no expression on the round face. The doctor's fingers were tender, probing around the wound. He applied antiseptic and covered it with a patch. Then he held a dark green bottle under the patient's nose and Howard stirred restlessly, groaning. His eyelids flickered open, but the pupils were dull, without recognition. He tried to speak, but there was only an inarticulate mumble.

With a sudden smile the doctor looked up at Elsa. "I think he's going to be all right, Miss Vaughn. Doubt if there's a fracture. Bad concussion at worst. But we should get him to a hospital at once for some pictures just to be on the safe side."

She was weak with relief. "I'll call an ambulance."

"How about the squad car?" asked Cullen. "I can clear traffic with the siren and shoot him right over."

The doctor nodded. "Excellent."

"Can he be moved without a stretcher?"

"I think so. The important thing is to get him to the hospital as quickly as possible."

Elsa said impatiently, "Let's get started."

"No, Miss Vaughn." The doctor shook his head. "You stay here. I want him kept absolutely quiet tonight. You can't possibly do him or yourself any good by sitting around in the hospital."

She consented reluctantly. "You'll keep me informed?"

"The moment the plates are developed."

Howard was struggling to sit up. His hand climbed to his scalp and he winced with pain at the contact.

"Easy, old man," the doctor said. "Here, give me a hand," he told Cullen.

They got Stark upright between them, supporting him to the door. He went along in the docile manner of a man who'd been drugged. Elsa watched, subdued and forlorn, until the elevator door closed behind them. Then she remembered Lieutenant Quentin's injunction and locked herself in. Back in the living room, she suddenly became aware of the damage. The sight of the broken records barely touched her. Another time she would have been speechless with anger; now it was only Howard who mattered. She wanted to cry, but she forced herself to concentrate on the meaning of the scene around her.

What could it mean? First the wanton destruction at Salz's apartment, and now here. Like the work of some psychopath who hated music. Suddenly her eyes were bright with conjecture. Orderly progression illuminated her thoughts as the wheels turned.

Salz's collection had been sabotaged. Why? Was it because some particular record had to be destroyed? Yes, of course! That was it. It had to be. Elsa's breath came faster. But the record had not been found. That's why her own place had been searched and her own collection wrecked.

Someone had reason to believe it was now in her possession. She gulped in excitement.

Rapidly the pieces fell into place. She had taken several records from Salz's studio. Among them was the one somebody wanted. But she had taken only her own and—

Her spine went rigid with sudden recollection and her pulse began racing. Elizabeth's prayer from *Tannhäuser*—at least, that's what the label said. But it wasn't Elizabeth's prayer from *Tannhäuser*. It wasn't even Elsa's voice. It was someone else in a very strange rendition of "Good-bye Forever."

She went down on her knees in a flurry of excitement, scrambling among the broken pieces, searching, rejecting. Suddenly she paused. She had left the record in her machine when she departed earlier this afternoon for the Met. She straightened and whirled toward the Capehart,* pawing the lid open. There it was on the turntable, still intact. The one place that hadn't been searched.

Elsa clicked the switch. The motor turned and tubes warmed. Breathing rapidly, she adjusted the needle. She was on the verge of something important; she could feel it in her bones.

And then it came, the conversion of electrical impulses into sound, the voice, off-key and overly dramatic, singing its tearful farewell. "Good-bye forever...."

Elsa listened. Her forehead screwed up in a fury of concentration. There was something vaguely familiar about that voice. It scratched at her memory. She tried to place it, summoning all the resources of a lifetime spent in training her ear. Suddenly the voice choked into silence. And then it spoke, a few broken words: "Good-bye, my darling. I'm going now, forever." They were punctuated by a sharp report, unmistakably the sound of a shot.

Elsa stiffened. Her hands flew to her mouth. She knew the voice. She had heard it before. It was Ivy Ecker.

She stood motionless, breathless, as comprehension dawned. Ivy hadn't been murdered; she had committed suicide.

Elsa turned, walking mechanically, like someone in a nightmare, and reached for the phone. She dialed Headquarters and asked for Lieutenant Quentin. But he wasn't in and they didn't know where he could be reached. She was a study in frustration, bursting with knowledge. She couldn't hold it. It was dangerous to hold it. She had to tell someone. Inspector Patrick, or the District Attorney. Someone. Her hand, reaching for the instrument again, halted in mid-air. It had started to ring, a rasping file

---

* A popular high-end record player of the day, including a feature that automatically turned over the record. With the development of the 33-rpm LP, the Capehart ceased to sell.

across her raw nerves. She snatched it up. Her spirits leaped as she heard the voice.

"Dave! Am I glad you called! If I can't talk to someone right away I'll explode. Can you hurry over? Where are you?"

"With Jane, halfway between Ridgefield and New York."

Her heart sank. "Oh, but that's miles away."

"What is it, Elsa?" The fever of excitement was contagious and he sounded tense. "What's up?"

She told him she knew what had happened to Ivy, adding breathlessly, "And I think I know who killed Rudolf Salz and Hilda Semple. It—"

She heard the noise behind her and whirled. A man was crouching near the wall where he'd picked up the telephone cord. An overwhelming rush of panic clutched her throat. He looked at her, not smiling, his face blank and gray, like a mask of papier-mâché. A vein kept throbbing erratically in his temple. His eyes, deep in their sockets, were empty of expression.

"You!" Elsa gasped. "Oh, my God!"

His hand jerked convulsively and the telephone cord ripped away from the wall with a crunching sound, its frayed ends loosely dangling.

"Yes," Karl Ecker said in a dead voice. "Me."

She cowered back against the sofa. "How did you get in?" she whispered.

He answered mechanically, like a man under a hypnotic spell. "I was here all the time, hiding in a closet, ever since you came home."

Elsa thought: Howard must have walked in on him, and then—She was afraid she was going to be sick, but the fear which froze her stomach prevented it. There was no human emotion at all in Ecker's face.

She swallowed painfully. "You knew I had the record, didn't

you, Karl?" Of course he knew. It had been playing when he phoned earlier today to tell her about the offer from Bayreuth.

"Yes," he nodded. "And I knew that sooner or later you would recognize Ivy's voice and guess that she had committed suicide."

"But why did you do it, Karl? You came home from Philadelphia and found her. Why did you make it look like murder?"

His voice was lifeless. "I needed the money. Double indemnity on her insurance. It looked so easy. All I had to do was throw the room in disorder and conceal the gun and jewels." He rubbed fingers across his temple in a meaningless gesture. "Poor Ivy! She'd been brooding about her voice. And then, one night she followed me when I went out to meet Edwina." His shoulders jerked convulsively. "I even looked for a suicide note. But I never thought of a record."

Elsa took a careful breath. She said, "Rudolf Salz found it, didn't he, Karl?" She spoke very quietly, very simply, as though she were trying to soothe an unhappy child.

He nodded apathetically. "Yes. Rudolf came to see me one day when I was under the shower. I hadn't noticed the record; it was still in the machine. He turned it on and knew right away what it was. He took it away."

"And started to blackmail you."

"Yes. He played it for me over the telephone and asked for money. I had to give it to him. I had no choice. He was bleeding me white."

The compression around Elsa's chest was suffocating. She was breathing through her mouth. "Did you have to *kill* him, Karl?"

"What else could I do?" His voice was petulant. "There was too much at stake. Salz kept threatening me. I had concealed evidence. I had defrauded an insurance company. He said it meant jail and disgrace. He said it would ruin my career." For a moment the drugged expression fell away and his face was suddenly filled with rage. "Salz was right. I know what scandal can do to a man's career. I was not willing to take the risk. So Salz had to die. I knew that months ago. When he came to my dressing room and offered me a drink I had the bottle ready."

Elsa saw his thick fingers flexing and unflexing at his sides. She said, still quietly, still soothingly, "Then you went to his studio, looking for the record."

He nodded, almost smiling. "You see, *Liebchen*, I am not all bad. I could not leave Jane tied up all night and so I called Quentin."

But he hadn't found the record and Elsa knew why. Because Salz had disguised it with a label bearing her name. So Karl had destroyed indiscriminately, and then his whole world collapsed. He phoned Elsa and heard it playing in her apartment. At any moment she might remember. The suspense must have been excruciating. He could not afford to wait. Time was running out. And now there was even more at stake because he had already killed a man. It explained his desperation, the wanton recklessness of firing a shot into her dressing room.

"Hilda was killed by mistake, wasn't she, Karl?"

Something like pain flickered in his eyes. He squeezed his temples between two fingers. The sound of his voice dwindled as he spoke. "I did not recognize her. I was too nervous, in too much of a hurry, and I only opened the door a little crack..."

In his own peculiar way he had been fond of Hilda, and Elsa understood why there had been so much emotion in his voice that afternoon when he had sung Tristan. And then she remembered something else.

"Why did you plant the jewels in Stanley DeBrett's garage?" she asked.

His brow wrinkled in perplexity, as if the answer must be obvious. "Because I would do anything to protect my career. Stanley was already under suspicion. He was the most logical victim."

She shrank away in revulsion. The pity and sorrow she had felt for him was gone. "You would even sacrifice an innocent man!" she said.

"Read the newspapers, Elsa. Our statesmen are always sacrificing innocent men on the altar of their ambitions. I am a realist. I learned about life in a hard school—the opera houses of Europe. One must be ruthless to get ahead." He smiled at her. "Between myself and Stanley DeBrett the choice was very limited. The fact is, I had him in mind from the beginning."

Elsa could detect a change in his voice, a faint note of boastfulness. "When I found Ivy, I guessed at once that she had taken the gun from her brother's desk. That is why I put it back. If it ever came too close to me I could steer the police in his direction. And later I let him lend it to me, in front of witnesses, of course." A chuckle whispered in his throat. "I even reported it stolen because I knew I would have to use it again. That seemed wiser than buying a new one that might later be traced back to me."

He leaned forward and deep furrows appeared in his brow. "I'm talking too much," he said with sudden harshness. He drew in a rasping breath that filled the huge barrel chest and he lifted his thick hands away from his sides. There was a yellow glow behind the blankness of his eyes.

Elsa felt beads of perspiration gather across her forehead in cold stigmata. "Karl!" she whispered. "Listen, please—"

He was moving toward her with the lumbering clumsiness of a bear. "There is no other way, Elsa. I'm sorry, but it's you or me...."

His hands reached out. Elsa felt her heart jump frenetically against her ribs. She wanted to scream. She tried to scream. All that came out was an inarticulate whimper. Her throat was frozen, paralyzed with terror. She put her hands up in a reflexive gesture of self-preservation, but Karl Ecker knocked them aside like twigs. His blunt, spatulate fingers circled her throat. She felt the steel bank closing around her throat with a pain that brought blinding tears to her eyes. The room tilted and slid sideways and began to darken as his weight bore down.

She was dimly aware of a sudden noise, the grind of metal, and a muffled yell. The thunder of a shot left her ears ringing. She felt Ecker's body jerk erect with the dreadful smack of a bullet. He shook in a convulsive spasm and his fingers fell mercifully away from her throat. She opened her eyes and saw him begin to topple, slowly at first, with his eyes glazed, going around in a half circle, like a building whose foundation has been pulled out.

The room was raw with silence, acrid with the smell of cordite. Lieutenant Quentin advanced toward the fallen man and looked down at him expressionlessly. A tendril of smoke was curling lazily away from the gun in his hand.

He stooped over and touched Ecker's throat with two fingers. Then he straightened slowly and looked at Elsa.

"Unconscious from shock. He'll live."

She spoke through parched lips. "You heard?"

"Enough to strap him in the Ossining broiler."*

His face was tired and his arm heavy as he reached for the telephone. When he saw the torn wire he cursed softly and headed for the door.

---

* Ossining, New York, was the home of the notorious Sing Sing Correctional Facility. New York applied the death penalty (the "electric chair") to heinous crimes until 1984—hence the "Ossining broiler" reference.

CHAPTER TWENTY-SEVEN

The room was strangely peaceful. They had taken Karl Ecker to Bellevue* under police guard. Lieutenant Quentin stood near the window, looking complacent for the first time in several days. A glass of sherry had restored some of the color to Elsa's cheeks but she was still a little jittery.

"It's all over now," Quentin told her. "You can relax now."

"Thanks to you, Lieutenant. You always seem to arrive on time. You must be psychic."

"No, ma'am. Cullen phoned me from the hospital after he delivered Stark. I burned his ears plenty for leaving you alone and raced over myself. I got a passkey on the way up and when I heard voices I opened the door as far as the chain would allow and listened. I'd like you to fill in a couple of details."

In a few minutes the story was told and Quentin regarded her in frank admiration. He said, "Any time you quit the Met I'll get you a job on the force. As a matter of fact, I was beginning to concentrate on Ecker myself after you left Headquarters this

---

* Bellevue Hospital, in New York, is the oldest public hospital in America and was the largest patient facility in New York. While popularly associated with its famous psychiatric hospital, it was in fact a general hospital and a frequent first stop for emergency care.

evening. I knew it had to be someone connected with the opera. If an outsider had killed Semple he would have left immediately and taken the gun with him. But it was ditched backstage by someone who couldn't leave, who had to stay for the performance. A simple process of elimination pointed to Ecker. At least, that's the way I reasoned it."

Elsa said, "I'm still a little confused. Who was responsible for turning on those gas jets?"

"Ecker."

"But why? I hadn't found Ivy's record yet. He was in no danger from me at that time."

"True," Quentin said. "And that's why he left the window open in the bedroom—because he did the thing with no homicidal intent. We got pieces of it from Ecker while we were loading him into the ambulance. He was a little delirious. You yourself had told him about our theory that the poisoned liquor was meant for you, not Salz. He merely hoped to sustain the illusion, to convince us that Salz was killed by mistake, hoping it would deflect the investigation. He was tossing a little mud into our eyes. He didn't want us prying too deeply into Salz's affairs. So he drugged your sherry and depressed the latch when he left, making it possible for him to come back later."

Elsa nodded slowly. It was clearing up, but she had one more question. "How did Salz get hold of my liquor bottle?"

"He took it from your dressing room. Salz was behind those earlier attacks. He dropped a hint or two to Ecker about it when he was drunk. He said he was going to put Hilda Semple in your place at the Met. As the owner of half her contract, it would increase his income. He was probably nosing around your dressing room looking for some way to keep you from performing when he saw the bottle and he couldn't resist the impulse to take it. Somebody must have scared him off before he could do anything else. The man had no scruples, no scruples at all. He had become money-hungry."

Elsa was looking past him into the distance. "It's not so hard to understand, Lieutenant. Rudolf Salz had tasted fame, great fame, then suddenly he had nothing. No voice, no material possessions. He had been very vain and now he desperately needed something to bolster his ego. He needed a sense of power. Money was the thing that could give it to him. He went after it wherever he could, blackmailing Ecker, blackmailing Mrs. DeBrett, using any means to increase Hilda's earning power. Deep inside, he was a lost soul...."

"Don't waste your pity, Miss Vaughn. There's too much evil in the world."

The bell rang. Someone was holding a finger on the button. Quentin went to the door and opened it, and saw Dave Lang's wild-eyed, haggard face. The words tumbled out.

"What's happened? I tried to reach you. I was talking to Miss Vaughn on the phone and the damn line went dead. Somebody was here in her apartment and I couldn't—"

"Whoa!" Quentin met the words and stopped them with an upraised palm. "Slow down, son."

Jane DeBrett, looking pale and tense, stood behind him. She was trying to peer over his shoulder when they heard the cry. It was Brünnehilde's war cry, the song of the Valkyries, reverberating triumphantly through the apartment, and all three of them jumped.

Dave suddenly grinned, and Jane's face was glowing. She ran past them into the living room, throwing herself at Elsa. The two men followed and waited. "It's all over," Elsa said. "You're just in time for dessert."

"Will somebody please bring us up to date?" Dave begged.

And so the story was told once more. Jane swung toward Quentin, her voice exultant.

"Then Dad is clear! Will he be released? Can we get him now?" Quentin nodded, smiling.

"Let's go." She was tugging at Dave's sleeve, like a happy, impatient child. "See you later, Elsa."

But Elsa was throwing a coat over her shoulders.

"We're all leaving," she said. "Lieutenant Quentin is driving me to the hospital to see Howard. And you're not to spare the siren either, Lieutenant."

It was a fast-moving convoy. They were in the elevator going down when Elsa began to chuckle. The chuckle grew to a laugh. The laugh swelled and echoed and they watched her in amazement until the spasm passed and she was drying her eyes.

"What brought that on?" Dave asked.

Elsa caught her breath. "It just occurred to me what an awful lot of time we wasted. We should have known the truth from the beginning."

"How?" demanded Quentin.

"Because of something my very first singing teacher told me. She was a wise old woman. She said, 'Elsa, no matter what happens, never trust a tenor.'"

A NOTE ABOUT
THE AUTHOR*

Helen Traubel has been called "the greatest Wagnerian soprano singing today" and "the finest singer, male or female, in the world today." The Associated Press, in its poll of member newspapers, unanimously selected her "the woman of the year in music" two years in succession, the first such event in history. In the career she chose when she was thirteen, she has won for herself a truly exalted position in the world of music.

But this does not wholly explain the hold she has on the public imagination. Her simplicity, her unconventionality, her utter lack of the professional snobbism and temperament that so often affect great artists—it is these qualities that have made her one of the best-known figures of our times and one of the best beloved.

Miss Traubel is as American as blueberry pie. She is a passionate baseball fan; is, in fact, a stockholder of the St. Louis Browns, the American League Club of her home town. One of the sorrows of her life is that she cannot go to many games because she roots so intensely and so vocally that she might damage her voice. She loves to cook and

---

* Published on the dustjacket and as an appendix to the first edition (1951).

to shop. She loves her occasional television appearances, in which she can play straight man for Jimmy Durante and convulse millions of listeners with her enormous, infectious laugh.

She loves mystery stories. In 1950 she decided to try her hand at writing one. It was a very amusing novelette, The Ptomaine Canary, and its warm reception, when it was serialized in newspapers all over the world, encouraged Miss Traubel to write a full-length book, which had to be called, inevitably, The Metropolitan Opera Murders.

READING GROUP GUIDE

1. Do you think that an artistic environment like the Metropolitan Opera naturally leads to eccentric characters such as those that appear in Traubel's book? Or did that seem artificial or made-up?

2. Did Traubel's numerous references to the opera repertoire and other things known only to opera aficionados make the book more enjoyable for you?

3. Critics called the mystery elements of the book "second-rate." Did plotting weaknesses affect your enjoyment of the book?

4. The novel was ghostwritten by Harold Q. Masur, a man with a background writing "hard-boiled" mysteries with a tough protagonist. Do you think that Masur's style infected the book? Or do you have the sense that this was a real collaboration?

5. How do you feel about the ethics of "ghostwritten" books? Should a celebrity acknowledge the work of a professional

writer? Or is that unimportant to your enjoyment of a book?

6. Did any of the characters' attitudes in the book seem dated or unique to the post–World War II era?

FURTHER READING

BY HELEN TRAUBEL:

The Ptomaine Canary. New York: AP Newswire, 1950. Originally serialized in more than two hundred newspapers.

St. Louis Woman. In collaboration with Richard G. Hubler. New York: Duell, Sloan and Pearce, 1959. Traubel's autobiography.

BY HAROLD Q. MASUR:

Bury Me Deep. New York: Simon & Schuster, 1947.

Suddenly a Corpse. New York: Simon & Schuster, 1949.

You Can't Live Forever. New York: Simon & Schuster, 1951.

So Rich, So Lovely, and So Dead. New York: Simon & Schuster, 1952.

The Big Money. New York: Simon & Schuster, 1954.

Tall, Dark and Deadly. New York: Simon & Schuster, 1956.

The Last Gamble. New York: Simon & Schuster, 1958.

Send Another Hearse. New York: Random House, 1960.

The Name Is Jordan. New York: Pyramid, 1962. Short stories.
Make a Killing. New York: Random House, 1964.
The Legacy Lenders. New York: Random House, 1967.
The Attorney. New York: Random House, 1973.
The Broker. New York: St. Martin's Press, 1981.
The Mourning After. New York: Raven House, 1981.

SIMILAR WORKS:

Francis, Dick. *Dead Cert.* London: Michael Joseph, 1962.
Lee, Gypsy Rose. *The G-String Murders.* New York: Simon
    & Schuster, 1941.
Sanders, George. *Crime on My Hands.* New York: Simon &
    Schuster, 1944.
Tillotson, Queena Marian. *Murder in the Opera House.* New
    York: E. P. Dutton, 1934. Written as Queena Mario.
Truman, Margaret. *Murder at the Library of Congress.* New
    York: Random House, 1999.

RELATED RESOURCES IN THE LIBRARY OF CONGRESS MUSIC DIVISION:

Helen Traubel Collection, 1920–1970. The collection
    includes Traubel's annotated music scores,
    photographs, scripts, clippings, correspondence, and
    scrapbooks documenting her career. https://lccn.loc
    .gov/2014571137.
Charles Jahant Collection of Photographs of Opera
    Singers, late nineteenth–late twentieth centuries. The
    collection contains many photos of Traubel and her
    contemporaries. https://lccn.loc.gov/2013572132.
Jessye Norman Papers, 1969–2018. Like Traubel, Norman

was an American opera singer who specialized in the operas of Richard Wagner, which is still a rarity. https://lccn.loc.gov/2016570619.

Albert Schatz Collection, 1541–1900. This is a comprehensive collection of opera librettos from the beginning of opera in the sixteenth century to the end of the nineteenth century, which encompasses most of the repertoire performed by Traubel and at the Metropolitan Opera. https://lccn.loc.gov/2016570576.

Leonard Bernstein Collection, circa 1900–1995. American conductor and composer Bernstein collaborated with Traubel on many occasions and his collection includes photographs of her. https://lccn.loc.gov/2009536078.

ABOUT THE AUTHOR

Helen Traubel as Brünnehilde in *Die Walküre*.
(Traubel Collection, Music Division, Library of Congress)

Helen Traubel (1899–1972) was born in St. Louis, Missouri, the child of Otto and Clara Traubel. Her father was a pharmacist, and her mother, a local concert singer. Helen studied singing in

St. Louis and debuted as a concert singer with the Saint Louis Symphony Orchestra in 1923. In 1926, the Metropolitan Opera offered her a contract in New York City, but Traubel declined, wishing instead to pursue her career as a concert singer. It was not until 1937 that she accepted a role at the Met. With two sopranos already established there—Kirsten Flagstad and Marjorie Lawrence—Traubel did not fit an immediate need of the Met, but when Flagstad returned to Norway during World War II and Lawrence's health failed, Traubel was able to step into the role of lead soprano. After 1941, she was the leading Wagnerian soprano of the company. Though she loved Italian opera, she never performed in a suitable role and was forced to include that repertoire only in her concert recitals.

After appearing frequently in USO-sponsored shows for the troops during World War II, Traubel decided that singing in venues distant from the opera stage also had value. She became a frequent performer on radio[*] and television (including starring in a failed sitcom pilot and appearing in an abridged production of *The Mikado* with Groucho Marx) as well as in nightclubs. By 1946, she was earning well over $200,000 per year from her opera and concert appearances and recording sales.[†] In 1953, Rudolph Bing, the manager of the Met, felt that she was cheapening her talents and forbade such popular appearances; however, calling Bing a snob, Traubel declined to renew her contract with the Met. She appeared in a Rodgers and Hammerstein musical on Broadway (*Pipe Dream*), and though it failed, her fame increased. Traubel also appeared in cameos in various films, and

---

[*] Traubel had her own half-hour show between 1936 and 1937, and in the 1940s she was a regular on Fred Allen's Sunday evening show. She was also a frequent guest on NBC Radio's "Monday Night of Music."

[†] Jim Cox, "Helen Traubel," *Musicmakers of Network Radio* (Jefferson, NC: McFarland, 2012), 319.

she is honored with a star on the Hollywood Walk of Fame for her contributions to the recording industry. She even had a rose variety named after her, introduced by hybridizer Herbert C. Swim in 1951. "Finally," writes Jim Cox in his short biography of Traubel, "and this may have been the best thing about her by allowing her to branch into so many demonstrable passions: she would be happy to form a brigade around her of folks who never took themselves too seriously... Traubel maintained an ability to laugh as powerfully as she sang, even when it meant poking fun at *her*."* In 1959, she penned an autobiography titled *St. Louis Woman*.† She retired in the mid-1960s to care for her husband, her former business manager William L. Bass. Traubel died of a heart attack in Santa Monica, California, on July 28, 1972, and is buried in the Westwood Village Memorial Park Cemetery in Los Angeles, along with stars like Marilyn Monroe, Walter Matthau, Jack Lemmon, and the publisher Hugh Hefner.

---

* Cox, "Helen Traubel," 313.

---

† In collaboration with Richard G. Hubler.